WARNING

This book contains sexually explicit scenes and adult language. It may be considered offensive to some readers. This book is for sale to adults ONLY.

* * * * * * * * * * * * * * * * * *

Please store your files wisely where they cannot be accessed by underage readers.

ISBN-13: 978-1773500553
ISBN-10: 1773500554

Other books by Shyla Starr:

<u>Tenacious Billionaire BWWM Romance Series</u>

Adalia is too proud to accept help from the billionaire playboy, Trent Dawson. How long can she maintain her resolve? The bank is at her heels to repossess her business. To make matters worse, Adalia finds suspicious evidence of Trent's philandering ways. She must determine whether to trust Trent with the fate of her business and her heart.

<u>Elusive Billionaire Romance Series</u>

Billionaire Hendrick is trying to repair his company's image by putting in some volunteer work, building a school and hospital for the impoverished children in Africa. There, he meets a beautiful African American volunteer, Jocelyn. They hit it off right away but does she belong in his world?

<u>Lonely Billionaire Romance Series</u>

Tricia was hired to care for billionaire John's wife, who is dying. An unlikely romance emerges after his wife, Rebecca, gives John permission to pursue his happiness after she is gone.

<u>Ardent Billionaire Romance Series</u>

Deirdre doesn't know what to make of the gorgeous man that seems to be interested in her. His name is Parker Walters and he seems friendly enough. There is just something off about him. Why is he trying the hide the fact that he is the heir to his father's billion dollar software empire?

<u>Fervent Billionaire BWWM Romance Series</u>

Alexandra had never been with a white man before. She had seen William at the café before but she always kept her distance. It was unfortunate that their first chance meeting happened when she dropped her breakfast and spilled coffee all over his expensive business suit.

<u>Audacious Billionaire BWWM Romance Series</u>

Chante is torn between staying close to a man beyond her league, and fleeing from him to spare herself from a hopeless position. But she finds she is propelled into a place where she needs to confront her doubts and cast her fate aside to follow the dictates of her heart. Damned if she does and miserable is she doesn't, how will Chante face the events that will lead her to a place of pure happiness or to the pits of a broken heart?

Get the latest update on new releases from the author at:

https://shylastarr.com/newsletter/

This book is Part One of the "Persuasive Billionaire BWWM Romance Series"

1 - Love Invested

Stacey is trying to keep a handle on her life the best that she can. She is on the verge of losing her job and her apartment, while taking care of her sick grandmother. Her life takes an unexpected turn when she meets Charlie, who works for the construction company that is attempting to persuade her to move out of her home.

2 - Love Divested

After discovering that Charlie has a fiancée, Stacey's world has turned upside down. She cannot help but feel as if she is in over her head. Struggling with her job, her bills and her family, will Stacey be able to figure out how she can get her life straightened out?

3 - Love Reinstated

Stacey decides that she has to put Charlie behind her and move on with her life. As Stacey dates Tony and is pulled into his world, she slowly realizes that although she likes him, it might not be enough to brush aside her feelings for Charlie. Leaving everything behind, she lets herself get lost in the money and privacy that Tony brings to her.

4 - Love Confirmed

Stacey can't believe the turn of events in her life. After losing her grandmother and running away to Tony's private island, she was content to stick her head in the sand and forget her past. But a proposal from Charlie changes everything.

5 - Love Divine

Stacey must ensure she relaxes in order to keep her baby safe. But life is never that easy. Her new husband's father is bent on sabotaging their fledgling investment firm. To make things worse, her brother-in-law isn't content with just being in the background. Stacey finds herself wishing she could have the brothers patch things up.

Persuasive Billionaire BWWM Romance Series

Love Invested

Book One

By Shyla Starr

Copyright Revelry Publishing 2018

Table of Contents

Chapter One

"**THEY'RE ASKING** for the eggs to be cooked again."

"What? Those are fine!"

"What do you want me to do about it, Brad? The customer is complaining. Just make them again, alright? He wants the eggs overcooked, apparently."

Brad took the plate from Stacey's hand and returned to his grill, grumbling loudly. Stacey wiped the sweat from her brow and turned around, getting ready to head back out onto the floor of *Papa's Grill and Diner*.

It was the middle of the day in mid-summer, which made the sweltering kitchen unbearable. Stacey was glad to leave the kitchen even if it meant dealing with a couple of jerk customers.

Back in the dining area, she looked around. She had only one couple in her section. They were older, with their shoulders hunched over and beady eyes pointed toward the kitchen. The woman hadn't touched her sandwich, probably waiting for the man to get his eggs back before digging in.

There was only one other waitress, Maria, working, and she was in the corner, texting on her phone. Their place wasn't exactly the hot spot of the city to eat during the best of times. During mid-day, it was more like a graveyard.

The woman motioned for Stacey to come over. She clenched her jaw, exhaled slowly and got ready for whatever ridiculous request the woman was going to make. This couple had been a hassle from the moment they were seated.

"How can I help you?" she asked, plastering a smile on her face.

The woman scowled, "Where are my husband's eggs?"

"They're making him a fresh batch right now."

"Tell them to hurry up!" the woman snapped.

The husband sat there silently, playing with the edge of his napkin. But he nodded at Stacey as if to tell her he better get his eggs soon.

Stacey scurried back into the kitchen. It was mind-numbing if she let it get to her. How long had she been working here now? Four years? It was supposed to be a pit stop before she moved onto bigger and better things. She had been there, scraping by, instead of returning to college or working on making something more of herself.

No use in thinking about that now.

Brad handed her a plate of freshly cooked eggs. She walked back to the table and placed it in front of the man and his wife.

The man wrinkled his nose and said, "This will do, I suppose."

Stacey clasped her hands together and inquired as politely as she could muster, "Would you like more coffee?"

They grunted, and she gave them a fresh pot, making sure not to add it their bill. She was sure they would want something for free out of the egg fiasco. By the time the couple left, Stacey was ready for a break.

In the break room, she slipped off her shoes and rubbed her feet, wincing. Her shoes were cheap, and it showed after standing in them for more than a couple of hours. Her feet were killing her.

She checked her phone next. There was a voicemail from her sister. It was a rare event that her sister reached out to her and she was filled with dread listening to the message.

"Stacey, hey. It's your sister, Allison," she added for clarification as if Stacey wouldn't know her own sister's name. "Listen, call me when you can? I have a question to ask you. Well, more of a favor? But I need to talk to you first. Thanks, bye."

Stacey sighed as the message ended. Her sister wanting a favor never led to anything good. *If she wants money, she can forget it.* There was no cash to give Allison. There were barely any funds for Stacey.

A small TV in the break room played the news. The image was grainy but she could just make out the weatherman talking about rain later on in the evening. *Great.* She made a mental note to make sure the roof didn't leak all over everything when she got home from work. Last time it stormed, Stacey had to set out buckets to catch the drips.

She closed her eyes just for a moment. If she left them closed for too long, she would fall asleep on the spot. It felt as if there was always something to do. She finished one thing, and another task popped up in its place. Maybe that was how it would always be.

"Wake up, sleepyhead."

Stacey opened her eyes to see Amanda stepping into the break room.

"You work today?" Stacey asked, surprised, wondering why they needed another waitress working during such a slow day.

"Nah, I left my wallet here last night in my locker. I was so tired after closing, it just slipped my mind." Amanda walked over to her locker and glanced back at Stacey. "You okay?"

"Yeah, just tired."

"Looks dead here. I'd be tired too," Amanda remarked as she opened up her locker.

"Yeah, it's pretty boring."

Amanda paused in front of her open locker, grabbed her wallet, and tucked it into her purse. When she turned back around, she had a strange look on her face. Stacey sat up straighter.

"What?"

Amanda hesitated and then sat down on the wooden bench. Stacey could see the purple circles under Amanda's eyes. Although they both worked full time at the restaurant, Amanda also attended college. She was probably just as tired as Stacey.

"I heard something. Probably just a rumor. I don't know. I wasn't going to tell anyone but—"

But I know how much you need this job was the unfinished thought there.

"What is it?"

Amanda lowered her voice, "Heard at a class yesterday this place might close down."

"Who was talking about that in your class?" Stacey scoffed. "Especially about our little place."

"Well, I mentioned that I work here. I was in my accounting class, and we were doing a project. This kid in my group said that I should look for other work because this place is going to shut down. Especially with all those investment groups coming in here trying to revive the area."

Stacey scowled. Her neighborhood, which was predominantly black, had indeed been crawling with rich white men in suits lately. All of them wanted to knock down and rebuild her section of town. They wanted to make it new and fresh again. They wanted it to appeal to the elite, which naturally meant getting rid of anyone who was low income.

"Thanks for the heads up, Amanda, but one kid in a college class saying we're going to close doesn't mean we are going to."

"Maybe. But this place is always dead. How long do you think we can stay open like this?" She stood up. "Don't tell anyone I told you, okay? I'll see you later."

Stacey watched her go, suddenly feeling wide awake. Even though she had sounded confident to Amanda that they weren't going to close, the girl had a point. Business had been awful lately. How long would they really be able to stay open?

Maybe it was time to find another job. The only reason Stacey had stuck around there for so long was how flexible the hours were. Few places would accommodate Stacey like that. But if this place was going to close, she may have to put some applications out.

She sighed and rubbed her forehead, fending off a headache. Just another worry to add to her long list.

Chapter Two

Stacey closed the front door of her apartment softly. She crept into the living room. The TV was on, showing the weather report. Apparently, Stacey wasn't going to be able to escape from bad weather news today. The rain was rolling in. She was glad that she had beaten it in time.

"That you, Stacey?" came a voice from one of the other rooms.

Stacey headed down the cramped hallway and stopped in front of one of the doors. She pushed it open a little and peered inside. Her grandmother, Tina, was sitting up in her bed with a magazine in her lap. Her lamp was on next to her, giving her just enough light to read by. Her eyes looked a little glassy, and her fingers were curled around one of the magazine pages. Her mind had been slowly deteriorating for a couple of years now. Stacey wondered how long Tina had been staring at the same page.

"Hey, I figured you'd be asleep."

"Couldn't sleep. Joints ache. It's going to rain, isn't it?"

"Yeah, it is."

Stacey came into the room and sat down at the edge of the bed. The room smelled like mothballs mixed with perfume. There was no point in telling her that she had left the TV on. Tina would have probably forgotten she was even out in the living room at one point.

"How was your day, doll?"

"It was okay. How are you feeling? Were you okay here by yourself?" Stacey asked.

Tina smiled and replied, "Just fine, dear. Although I wouldn't mind some warm milk."

"Let me get you some," Stacey said as she got up.

She was almost at the door when Tina spoke, "Oh, someone came to the door today."

"You answered?" she asked with a sigh. "You know you should be resting, not answering doors."

"Well, he wouldn't go away."

"What did he say?"

Tina's face scrunched up as she tried to remember. Stacey watched with a stab of pain in her chest. It was so hard watching her grandmother like this. It was even harder leaving her alone during the day while she worked. She could barely afford doctors and medicine, so there was no way she could pay for a nurse or an assisted-living facility.

"I don't know, dear. What were we talking about?"

"You wanted warm milk."

"Ah, yes. That would be lovely," Tina replied and smiled at her.

Stacey returned the smile and went back to the living room. She turned off the TV and continued to the front door. There was a small table beside it where she had tossed her keys and hadn't noticed the envelope. It had her name typed on it.

Stacey didn't even have to open it to know what it was going to be. She picked it up and debated just throwing it out without reading it. But that could come back and bite her in the ass.

As she warmed up the milk, she opened up the letter and scanned it quickly. It was the same old shit. They were trying to vacate everyone from the building so they could knock it down. They probably wanted to build some high rise or something in its place.

This time, they were offering money. But it wasn't enough. Sure, they could take the money and could go. But between Stacey's debts, taking care of her grandmother, and then trying to find a place that was cheap enough for them to live, this money ultimately didn't help. There was no other place in the city that Stacey could afford that wasn't in a seedy neighborhood or by some noisy factory.

A headache she had been fending off all day came back with a vengeance. The panic that she tried to fight off at the same time also threatened to return. Where would they go? She didn't want to live in the slums.

She didn't want to put her grandmother in danger. On top of that, if the restaurant did close, she would be out of a job.

"When it rains, it pours," Stacey mumbled and shoved the letter back into the envelope.

She took the warm milk to Tina who was still on the same page of the magazine. She put it next to her on the night table and adjusted her pillows.

"Need anything else?"

"Oh, someone came to the door for you today," Tina repeated.

"Did they?"

"Yes. They were from that business group. The construction group."

Stacey pretended as if this was new information for her. "What did they want?"

"Just about the area. About improving it," Tina said, settling in with her milk.

Stacey doubted they would have told her grandmother anything. It was common knowledge, even among the people working in the company that hovered around there, that her grandmother was forgetful and not well. At least they had the decency not to harasses her.

"Well, thanks for letting me know."

Tina smiled and looked back down at her magazine. Stacey studied her for a few seconds and then slipped out of the room quietly. Sometimes, Tina forgot that anyone was there and would be startled by Stacey speaking. Best to leave her alone.

Back in the kitchen, she made herself a sandwich and sat down at the tiny dining room table. Then she remembered it might rain. Leaving the sandwich, she pulled buckets out of the closet and put them down where the roof sometimes leaked when it rained. With that finished, she was finally able to eat.

The rain started when she was halfway through her meal. It was a mean summer storm that rolled through hard. The lights flickered at one point, and Stacey wondered idly if they were going to lose power. She finished her sandwich, washed the plate, and sat down in the living room.

She could hear Tina snoring. Warm milk always helped her sleep, and once that woman was dozing, there wasn't much that could wake her. Stacey listened to the rain pounding against the roof. There was a soft dripping noise from the kitchen which meant the roof was leaking a little.

Not for the first time, Stacey tried to talk her way through the scenario of accepting the money and vacating the apartment complex. Surely, there had to be some place to move that was decent and affordable.

If the restaurant closed down, maybe she could work part-time at another restaurant at night and find a better job during the day. She had very little experience outside of waiting tables. But it wouldn't hurt to try to find an office job. Someplace that would give her work from nine to five so she could get extra hours during the evenings.

Right before Stacey fell asleep on the couch, she remembered she forgot to call her sister back. But she was too tired. Her sister would have to wait until the morning.

Chapter Three

After Stacey got out of the shower the next morning, she stopped in front of the floor-length mirror. She had originally bought it when she had been determined to lose weight, thinking it would have been a great way to see the changes in her body.

Now, as she stared at herself, she found nothing had changed. While she normally wore her black curly hair in braids or Bantu knots for work, she liked to keep it natural. Her body weight was also unchanged. The old *compliment* she always got reared its head.

"You're pretty for a plus-sized girl."

As if she wasn't pretty enough for a regular-sized woman. Just plus-sized. She groaned a little and considered getting rid of that damned mirror. She was dressing for work but wasn't looking forward to the double shift today. *Must get some coffee.*

Stacey yawned and went to check on Tina while she made her cheap coffee. Tina was still fast asleep and could stay like that for hours. Stacey moved the magazine from the bed and watched her sleep.

Her parents had died when she was young. They were killed in a car accident on the way back from a party. Stacey's grandparents had taken both her and Allison in. The elderly couple had done what they could to care for the girls. When her grandfather died from cancer two years ago, and Tina also grew ill, Stacey knew that she would take care of her as long as she could.

Now, watching her sleep, she felt guilty again at leaving her at home. Was Stacey doing a good job taking care of her grandmother? Barely scraping by, living in this shitty apartment—surely, there had to be more she could do to improve things.

Stacey blinked back tears. Growing emotional right now before work did her no favors. She would figure something out. She was a fighter, just like Tina.

She closed the front door behind her and locked it. Then she headed down the hallway. As she got close to the stairs, one of the apartment doors opened. Leon, a younger boy who had dropped out of high school a month ago, slouched in the doorway.

"Good morning," Stacey said.

"Hey. Those pricks were here again yesterday."

"Yeah, I heard."

He shook his head and then said, "They offered us money this time."

"Well, they really want us out of here. Prime real estate we're sitting on here."

"Mom says we should hold out for more money." He frowned. "Where're we gonna go, though? You even said it yourself. This place is the best we can get without ending up in the ghetto."

"Well, we'll figure it out, Leon," Stacey said trying to sound positive.

Leon narrowed his eyes at her as if he didn't believe her and shrugged. "I guess."

He slunk back into the apartment and closed the door without another word. Stacey felt bad about brushing him off, but she didn't know what else she could say. The last thing she wanted to do was tell him that he should be worried, and have his mom freaking out on her. Holding out for more money was a good idea, but it still didn't help them figure out where they were going to go.

She went down three flights of stairs. The elevator had been broken for two months now. Stacey doubted that it was going to be fixed at this point. It was just another thing the owners could use to try to get them to move out.

She reached the lobby, for lack of a better word, of the apartment complex. An old desk sat in one corner, left over from the days where there apparently used to be a security guard. There had never been one the entire time Stacey lived in the complex. Yet the desk remained as if to remind everyone that the place used to be nicer than its current state.

The tiles were cracked in places and in need of repair, but Stacey didn't notice them anymore. The mailboxes were against the other side of the wall. She had forgotten to check the mail last night and wanted to grab it before she left for the day.

Yet she hesitated. Leaning against the mailboxes was a man, and he had his phone out. It wasn't one of the old flip phones she normally saw around here but a smartphone with a giant screen. It looked more like a tablet than a phone. Expensive.

Her eyes scanned the figure in front of her. He was decked out in a suit that looked as if it was perfectly tailored to his body. There wasn't an inch of fabric that wasn't fitted to his movements. His tie was neat and looked expensive. His hair was slicked back, and he had fine stubble along his jawline.

Even though the man was undeniably handsome, there was no way that Stacey didn't know where he was from. From his suit to his phone to the casual way he was leaning against the mailboxes—*her* mailbox, she realized—it was clear that he was part of the construction company trying to make her and everyone else vacate the property.

Stacey cleared her throat. The man didn't look up. Irritation swept through her. She didn't bother to clear her throat this time.

"You're in my way," she announced loudly.

This finally got the man's attention. He looked up from his stupidly large phone, and he gave her an embarrassed smile.

"Sorry, miss." He moved to the side, allowing her access to her mailbox.

Stacey opened it up and slipped out two letters. She glanced at them and knew they were about overdue bills. The man was staring at her as if she was some sort of exhibit. It angered her.

"What? Don't have poor people in your company?"

The man's eyes widened slightly in surprise. *Take that*, Stacey thought vindictively. She was just in the mood to tell off anyone working for that construction company.

"My company?" he finally replied.

"Yeah, Lexington & Albert Construction. A subsidiary of Albert Investment Corp."

"You've done your homework."

"I try to when a company sweeps in here trying to kick us out of our homes," Stacey said, slamming the small mailbox door shut.

"Ah, well, that's not exactly it—"

"Please," she said, holding her hand up as if to ward him off. "Not this morning. I don't need to hear this bullshit speech yet again while I'm on the way to work."

A strange look flickered over the man's face. It looked almost as if he was amused. Of course, he was. What else could be more hilarious than watching the tenants of this small apartment complex struggle under the mighty foot of this construction company? It just irritated her more.

"You know, you and all your other companies that are circling around this area might think it is going to be great to rebuild here. But you have no idea what it will be like for us," she continued, pointing to herself and the stairs, "to find a place that is as decent as this."

"Decent?" the man scoffed. "No offense, miss, but I've seen what this place looks like. We're offering everyone here a fair sum to vacate."

"And go where? The slums? The ghetto? The only other place we can all afford is at the far end of the city, and you know what that's like." Stacey caught herself and shook her head. "Never mind. You probably don't. You're kicking us out to a section of the city that will eat us alive. All we have going for us are these shitty apartments. No, you're right. They aren't much. They're busted up, broken and tarnished. But they're ours. They keep us as safe as they can and keep us going. Think about that the next time you come down here to bother us."

She breezed past him without another word. Their shoulders brushed against each other as she walked by him. An electric shock fired through her all the way down to her toes. Stacey paused for just a moment to process what she had just felt. She shook it off, opened the front door of the apartment complex, and went out onto the street, slamming the door behind her.

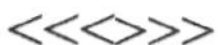

"Two coffees. Need anything else?" Stacey asked the elderly couple that had just sat down.

"No, not yet. Thank you, dear," the woman replied.

Stacey smiled and nodded, leaving them alone. She was on autopilot today. The restaurant was busier than usual for lunch, which was a welcome distraction from her own feelings. She couldn't help but regret how she had spoken to that man in the lobby. It wasn't that she worried about hurting his feelings. She was worried that he was going to go back to his boss and complain that the people in the apartment complex were openly hostile. What if it made things worse?

Stacey had let her irritation and emotions get the better of her. She had to keep them in check next time. Lashing out at some low-ranking company official wasn't going to fix anything.

In the kitchen, Amanda was yawning and pouring herself a cup of coffee. Amanda's fingers shook slightly, but noticeably.

"Girl, how much caffeine are you drinking?" Stacey asked her.

"Way too much," Amanda quipped, looking down at her hands. "I'm studying for a major biology test as well as putting all my work hours in."

Stacey leaned over and plucked the cup out of Amanda's hands.

"Hey, give that back!" Amanda protested.

Stacey shook her head. "Cutting you off. You're going to give yourself a heart attack. You're too young for that."

"Fine, fine." Amanda yielded and then leaned forward. "Maria called in sick today."

Stacey groaned, "Really?"

"Yeah. Just you and me until closing." She patted Stacey on the back. "You might want to keep that cup of coffee for yourself."

Stacey watched her go and looked down at the coffee. Gingerly, she took a sip and cringed. It was bitter and had been on the burner for too long. She dumped it out and began to make a new pot. She was surprised the elderly couple she had just served wasn't complaining.

"Stacey, hey. There you are."

She turned around to see her boss poking his head into the kitchen.

"William! Hi. Good morning."

"When the customers are settled in, will you come see me?"

"Sure," Stacey replied.

William, the owner of *Papa's Grill and Diner,* nodded and ducked out of the kitchen. A lump formed in Stacey's throat. She couldn't remember the last time he had wanted to speak to her directly. Whatever it was, she knew it wasn't going to be good.

The next few hours dragged by. Even though they were a bit busy for once, Stacey dwelled on whatever William wanted to discuss. By the time her break rolled around, her stomach was a knot of tightly wound anxiety.

She paused for a moment outside his office door, listening to hear if anyone else was in there, but there was just silence. She knocked twice and heard him tell her to come in, to which she obliged. The office, like the rest of the restaurant, had a theme that wasn't quite as identifiable as other places. It was as if William had tried to create a family friendly place with a western theme, but a few years ago thought that adding a few art-deco modifications would be a good idea. Now, the place looked like a fevered dream of the worst sort.

His office had the same sort of feel. Behind his desk was a giant cowboy hat on the wall. Yet the desk itself was modern-looking. There was hay in the corner that should have been swapped out two weeks ago. The paintings on the wall were sleek and full of silver lines and dark shapes.

"Close the door and have a seat," William said to her.

Stacey closed the door which only increased her anxiety, and sat down across from him. William was a very thin man who looked more like an accountant than a restaurant owner. His glasses were taped in the middle and rested on the edge of his nose. He was balding but tried to cover it up with a terrible comb-over. His suits were always a size too big for him. Even today, the cuffs of his shirt seemed to swallow up his hands. For a moment, Stacey pictured the man from this morning and how well his own suit fit compared to William's.

"I won't take up too much of your break."

"Oh, that's alright. Everything okay?" Stacey asked nervously, fiddling with a ring on her finger.

William pursed his lips and then leaned forward a little, "I wanted to tell you first. You've been here the longest, and it only seemed fair."

"You're closing, aren't you?" she blurted out.

William looked surprised and pushed his glasses higher up his nose. He blinked twice. Stacey waited for him to confirm what she already knew had to be true.

"Yes," he finally said.

It felt as if someone had punched her in the stomach. More bad luck upon bad luck. Her shoulders slouched forward, and she closed her eyes for a couple of seconds.

William continued, "I'm selling. You've noticed, I'm sure, how we haven't been doing too well. I'm bleeding money here, Stacey. I thought this place would be bigger than what it is. Ten years ago, who knows,"

He shook his head. "A decade is a good run. Especially for a family-owned restaurant."

"Who's buying this place?"

"Griffins."

"The restaurant chain? The ones that have an arcade where parents can shove their kids during meals?"

"Yes. They're knocking this place down—"

"And rebuilding," Stacey finished with a sigh. "Makes sense."

William took off his glasses and rubbed his eyes. "I know it's hard. You've been here the longest. I wish things would have turned out differently."

"How long do I have?"

"A month. We close in thirty days."

"A month," Stacey repeated. "Longer than I thought."

"I know once word gets out, everyone will quit. I'll give you as many hours as you want, Stacey, to cover for how short staffed we will be. I'll give you a recommendation letter for future jobs. I know it won't be easy," he said as he cleared his throat. "I know that Tina is ill, and this job gave you the flexibility to be with her when you could. I'm sorry."

"Well, thanks for letting me know first. It means a lot." She stood up quickly, suddenly desperate to get out of that small, strange office.

William nodded and said something, but she didn't hear him. She turned around and left with a wave, anxious to leave. Then she marched down to the bathroom in the break room and closed the door behind her tightly.

She fumbled for the light switch and stared at herself in the mirror. She wasn't sure exactly how she was feeling right now. Crappy, obviously. Panicked, certainly. Anxious, without a doubt. It felt as if the walls were closing in on her, and escape was impossible.

They were going to lose their home and end up in the slums or worse. Stacey was going to be out of a job at the end of the month if she didn't find something quickly. Her head throbbed with the promise of another headache. It was just one bad thing after another.

Amanda had told her, hadn't she? Just yesterday. Stacey had been so quick to blow her off, but she had been right. This entire section of town was going to be renovated. It was going to leave Stacey floundering, it would leave her in the dust.

Chapter Four

By the time work was done that night, Stacey would have given anything to sink into a hot bath until the water turned cold. But the bus was delayed in traffic due to a two-car accident on the road. She didn't get home until close to midnight.

The apartment complex was as quiet as a mouse by the time she reached it. There were only a few lights on. She climbed up the stairs to her home and looked around. The TV was off at least, which meant she hadn't been paying for that all day. Stacey slipped her shoes off with a sigh and went to check on Tina.

She was fast asleep, snoring a little. Stacey watched her sleep for a couple of minutes. She tried to digest what it would be like moving Tina to a new place and finding a different job. There were changes ahead—yet were any of them going to be positive?

Stacey went to her own room. It was small and could barely fit her bed, a dresser, and that mirror she detested. She changed into her pajamas and curled up in bed.

She had been anxious and thought she would be up all night with worry. But exhaustion won out, and she fell asleep in a few minutes. She had forgotten to brush her teeth.

<<◇>>

"There you go," Stacey said to her grandmother. "Do you want to read your magazine?"

"Not yet. I think I'll relax here for a few minutes."

"Terrific, I'll relax with you."

She sat down next to Tina and stared out at the area in front of them. Stacey had the day off, thankfully, and she wanted to spend it with Tina. There was a small yard at the back of the apartment complex that served as a garden or play area for the residents. Tina liked to sit in the sun and admire the view. It wasn't much of a view, Stacey secretly thought, but it made Tina happy and that was all she cared about in the end.

There was a breeze today which helped ward off the heat. They were under a tree which offered shade as well. Stacey had brought a book, but she wasn't sure if she would be able to focus on it today. Tina closed her eyes and hummed.

There was a sprawl of garden in front of them. A few of the residents tended to it although it looked badly in need of watering. Once they got the notices to vacate, the garden had fallen by the wayside, like so many other things it seemed. Two of the younger kids from the complex were climbing a tree on the other side of the park.

"Nice, isn't it?" Tina asked.

"Yeah. Very pretty," Stacey replied.

"What's bothering you?"

The question surprised Stacey. She had thought she had been masking her inner turmoil well enough to hide it from her grandmother. Tina seemed to sense this and smiled at her a little.

"Stacey, I have known you since you were just a little thing. I can tell when things are bothering you."

She was on the fence about how much to share with her grandmother. She didn't want to worry her. It was also easy to confuse her with too many details or things to remember. Sometimes, they would be mid-conversation and Tina would forget what they were discussing.

She didn't get a chance to reply. Tina spoke up again.

"Is it the man who came to the door yesterday?"

Stacey was surprised that she still remembered. "Yes."

"They want us out of here, don't they?" When Stacey nodded, Tina clicked her tongue against the roof of her mouth. "We'll figure it out."

"Yeah, we will."

Tina wrinkled her nose a little. "They want to rebuild the city, don't they?"

"Yeah. Make this area better for the rich folk."

"It's because we have the ocean over there," she replied, gesturing over to the west. "This area has too much potential. I assumed it would be sooner or later that we would get the interest of profit-seeking companies."

Stacey hadn't been to the ocean in ages. Even though they were so close to it, she had no interest in trying to find a bathing suit she felt okay in. Last time she had gone to the shore was back in high school where her boyfriend at the time had made such a cruel remark about her weight that sometimes it still bothered her.

"Yeah, you're right."

Tina opened her magazine and looked down at it. Stacey could see that her grandmother had lost interest in the conversation. She didn't want to press it further. She opened her own book, but the words seemed to float in front of her eyes without making sense.

It was then that a cry came out from the tree across the garden. Stacey looked up. One of the kids who had been playing was at the bottom of the tree, shouting up. A panicked voice was shouting back.

"Can you stay here alone for a second?" Stacey asked Tina, who nodded.

She hurried over to see what the fuss was about. As she got closer, she saw that the two kids were Zack and Kevin. They were brothers who lived on the second floor with their mom. She worked long hours, so she probably wasn't home.

"Hey, Zack," Stacey said to the first boy. "What's wrong?"

"Kevin is stuck," he said, pointing with his thin finger up to the tree.

"What?"

"Help me!" Kevin wailed as if he was going to fall to his death at any moment.

Stacey went to the base of the tree and peered up. High above her, she could see Kevin. He was clinging to one of the branches. He was awfully high up, way higher than he should have been. She sighed inwardly.

"You're going to be okay, so don't panic. Just hang on, alright?"

Kevin wailed in reply. Stacey turned to look back at Zack.

"Why did he climb so high?"

"He said Mom was at work and couldn't yell at us, so he wanted to see if he could reach the top. But now he's stuck." Zack turned to face Stacey. "You have to help get him down! Mom will kill us if he falls and breaks his leg or something stupid."

"We'll figure something out," Stacey said and looked back up the tree.

Kevin was sniffling loudly. Zack was shouting encouraging remarks to try to convince him to climb down on his own. Staring up at Kevin, Stacey tried to think of a way she could get him down safely. There was no way she could climb up there. She'd end up flat on her ass on the ground.

"Trouble?" A voice came from behind.

Stacey turned around. To her chagrin, it was the man she had lectured in the lobby the other day. He was wearing a different suit and looked the same as before, dapper. He slipped his phone into the pocket of his suit jacket.

Before Stacey could stop Zack, he was bounding up to the man and was telling him about Kevin being stuck up in the tree. The man went over to assess the situation. Kevin cried back in reply.

"I'll get him," the man said abruptly. "It's a manageable climb. The kid is just afraid to come back down."

"He could break his leg if he fell from that distance," Stacey said pointedly.

The man flashed her a grin. "Well, he won't fall then, will he?" He turned to look at Zack. "You said his name is Kevin?"

"Yes, sir."

"Kevin?" he called up the tree as he shrugged out of his suit jacket. "My name is Charlie. I'm coming up to get you, okay?"

Kevin made a little whimpering noise in response. Charlie's jacket hit the ground, and Stacey cringed. She was sure that jacket alone was hundreds if not thousands of dollars yet Charlie barely noticed as it fell onto a pile of dirt.

Before she could caution him, he began to scale the tree. For some reason, she had expected his climbing to be dismal, but he managed with ease. In what felt like a matter of moments he was halfway up the tree.

"Be careful," Stacey called up. The last thing she needed was the two of them toppling down to the ground.

She could hear Charlie talking to Kevin in a low voice. He was trying to soothe the boy. Next to her, Zack bounced nervously on the balls of his feet.

There was a shifting noise, and for one awful second, she swore the entire branch was going to crack underneath their weight. But Charlie was shimmying down the tree now, holding Kevin tightly with one arm.

Climbing down took longer than going up. After ten minutes, they landed safely on the ground. Charlie released Kevin, and Zack promptly went over and pushed his brother.

"Idiot! Mom would have flipped out!"

Stacey separated the two boys before they could start fighting. "Stop it, you two. Go inside. Wait for your mother to get home, okay? No more climbing trees for either of you." She hesitated for a moment. "And don't forget to thank Mr. Charlie for saving your miserable necks."

The boys mumbled their thanks. Both looked embarrassed for their stupidity. With an extra thank you from Kevin, they took off across the garden back toward the apartment. Stacey could see Tina flipping through her magazine from where she stood. She turned back to Charlie.

"Thank you for your help. I'm so sorry, but your shirt is dirty," she pointed out.

He had been wearing a white dress shirt underneath his suit jacket. There were dirt smears from the tree along the sleeves. He tried to brush them off, but they didn't budge.

"I'll clean it later," Charlie said with a shrug.

Stacey bent over and picked up his suit jacket. She thrust it toward him, trying to avoid his gaze. He took it from her and slipped into it. She wondered why he would wear it when it was so warm out today.

"Good thing I happened by," he said as he finished adjusting his jacket. "Kid would've been stuck up there for a while."

"We would have figured something out," Stacey said, automatically defensive.

Charlie grinned at her. It was a lop-sided grin, one that looked as if he was in on a private joke. Even if he did help her out with Kevin, he still worked for Lexington & Albert.

"Why are you hanging around here, anyway?" she asked.

"Business."

"Business," she repeated coldly.

"I don't think I caught your name?"

"That's because I didn't tell it to you."

Charlie grinned again. Her chest tightened at the sight of it, and she looked away from him over to her grandmother. It infuriated her that she found him attractive and charming.

"I need to get going," she said, determined not to look at him again. "Thank you again for helping Kevin."

As she turned around, eager to escape the way he made her feel, Charlie said, "It's Stacey, right?"

She turned back in surprise, "How did you know that?"

"The boy told me. Up in the tree. He said you were going to help him and he was glad you were around."

Stacey shrugged. She didn't know what to say in reply. Anything else could possibly drag out the conversation, and she wanted to put some distance between her and this fellow with his fancy suit and inviting grin.

"See you around, Stacey," he called after her.

She scowled but kept on walking.

Chapter Five

By the time Stacey made it to work the next day, the other employees had been told that the restaurant was closing at the end of the month. Three people quit on the spot, leaving them just as short-staffed as William had predicted. Her five-hour shift quickly turned into a ten-hour one.

She was by herself until Amanda came into work that evening. When Stacey saw her, she dashed over and gripped her arm.

"Please tell me you aren't quitting just yet. I swear, if you do, William will have me work every day, all day until we close."

"I'm not leaving," she promised. "I'm on this sinking ship with you."

Stacey sighed in relief, "Great. At least someone is sticking around."

"I have a job lined up at the end of the month already. My friend's dad needs someone to work as a receptionist in his real estate office."

"That's great. I'm glad you have somewhere to go."

"What about you? Any ideas?"

"No. Not yet, anyway."

"I'll let you know if I hear of anything you'd be a good fit for." She put her hair up in a ponytail. "I should head out there."

Stacey trailed after her, lost in thought. She needed to start looking for work, but how, when she was pulling double shifts? It would be a disaster to find herself unemployed at the end of the month. She was so preoccupied about her work situation that she didn't notice until she went over to take a new table's drink order that her customers included Charlie.

He was sitting at the table along with two other men. One of the men looked ancient. His face was lined with wrinkles, and he was hunched over in the booth, staring at the menu. The other man was younger and was sitting very stiffly. He had red hair that was askew from the wind outside. He flattened it down when he saw Stacey approach. Then there was Charlie who had sat alone on the other side of the booth.

His hair wasn't slicked back and his clothes were a bit more casual than the last two times she had seen him. When he saw her, he smiled brightly as if they were old friends. She hoped that he would pretend he didn't know her.

Stacey's heart raced unexpectedly. Why should she care that Charlie was there, in her restaurant? He was nothing to her. She decided to be professional and simply asked the party what they wanted to drink. Charlie ordered water while the other two men ordered tea.

She left quickly, hoping they wouldn't notice her blushing. She had no idea why she should be embarrassed. Despite her best efforts to avoid eye contact, she glanced back at the booth on the way to the kitchen.

Charlie was watching her go. Under the table, he wiggled his fingers at her to say hello. She felt her face flush even deeper and turned away. What was that guy's deal, anyway? She had made it clear from their first meeting that she thought he was a slime ball. Even if he was good looking, that was no excuse.

She almost ran into Amanda who was on the way out of the kitchen. *Good looking?* Since when had she even looked at Charlie close enough to think that he was good looking? He was probably some low-level grunt at that construction company, determined to kick everyone out of their homes. It didn't matter what he looked like. He was the enemy.

When she returned to serve the drinks, she avoided looking at Charlie completely. Stacey could feel his eyes on her as she took their food orders. Her hands were sweaty, and she almost dropped her pen.

It felt like they took ages to eat their meals once it arrived. Every time she stopped by to check on them, she wanted to hide her face. She couldn't pinpoint why she felt so weird around him but was relieved when Charlie and his companions left.

By that time, the so-called dinner rush had calmed down. Amanda had two tables in her section. Stacey heard the front door of the restaurant open. The hostess had quit this morning so Amanda and Stacey had been taking turns seating people but it wasn't as if there were a lot of customers, anyway.

She looked up to see who had come in when her mouth went dry. Charlie had come back inside and was sauntering up to her.

"Forget something?"

"Nope."

"What do you want then?" She crossed her arms as if to ward him off.

Charlie didn't seem to notice. "I was wondering if you'd go out with me."

Stacey stared at him, certain she hadn't heard him correctly. "What?"

"You and me," he gestured between the two of them, "on a date."

"Why would I want to go on a date with you?"

Charlie ran his fingers through his brown hair and smiled. "Right, you don't like me, is that it?"

"You work for the company that is trying to kick us out of our homes."

Something flickered across his eyes. It was only a second. Stacey wasn't even sure if it had really been there or if she had imagined it. But then his easy-going smile returned, and he shoved his hands into his pockets.

"Gonna blame a man for what his work is doing? I have bills to pay too. Wouldn't you do it if it meant you could make rent that month?"

Stacey hesitated. He had a point, but she still didn't want to admit it. He waited for her to reply, seemingly unbothered that it was taking her a few seconds to think it through. She inwardly groaned. Despite the racial difference, he was good looking, and she had been thinking about him lately, hadn't she? But how would that work out? They were worlds apart in many other things.

But it had been ages since she had been on a date. The last time she went on a date, the guy told her that they couldn't go anywhere public because he didn't want to be seen with a *girl like her*. Stacey didn't bother to ask if that meant her weight or her skin color because she left promptly afterward.

"Fine," she conceded.

"Great. What's your phone number? Does tomorrow night work for you?"

"No. I'm working a double."

"No problem." He handed her his phone—that giant smartphone again. "Put your number in there."

Stacey held the phone gingerly as if she was afraid she was going to drop it. The contact screen stared back at her. She supposed it was touch screen, but she had never had a phone like this in her life.

"I don't wanna hold this thing," she admitted. "Is this even a phone? Looks like you have a computer strapped to your ear."

Charlie laughed. The sound of his chuckle made her skin break out in goosebumps. He took the phone from her, and she gave him her number verbally instead. Then he slipped his phone into his pocket.

"I'll text you."

"Call me. I have to pay for texting."

"Alright. I'll call you then. We'll figure out a time. Goodnight, Stacey."

He nodded his head at her and turned around. She watched him leave, feeling slightly shocked by the sudden turn of events.

"Wow, who was that?" Amanda said, slinking up next to her. "He had a cute butt."

When Stacey got home that night, she was looking forward to curling up in bed and sleeping. Not only had the day been long and her feet ached, but the fact that she was apparently going on a date with Charlie had left her with mixed emotions. She was surprised that she wanted to go on a date with him and was looking forward to it. Was it wrong of her to see him when he worked for Lexington & Albert construction?

When she arrived at her apartment and went to unlock the front door, she saw that the door was already unlocked. With trepidation, Stacey opened it and looked inside. She was expecting something terrible to have happened.

Instead, her sister, Allison, was lying on the couch. She had a bag of chips on her stomach and was watching TV. When she saw Stacey, she sat up quickly.

"Finally, you're home."

"What are you doing here?" Stacey asked bluntly.

Allison got to her feet, brushing the crumbs off her t-shirt. Stacey hadn't seen her sister in a long time. They looked like polar opposites. Her skin was a bit lighter than Stacey's, and she was rail thin. Her t-shirt looked as if it wasn't even hers because it was too big on her. Knowing her sister, Stacey thought it was safe to assume that it wasn't Allison's t-shirt but one of her boyfriend's. Her sister's hair had been curled, and the tresses rolled down across her shoulders, framing her heart-shaped face.

"I tried calling you," Allison protested. "You never called me back."

"So, you just show up? That's nice of you to check in personally, but I'm fine. We're both fine," she said, meaning Tina.

"I need a favor."

"Of course, you do," Stacey mumbled as she walked past Allison to get to the kitchen.

Her sister trailed after her. The last person that Stacey wanted to see, to be honest, was her sister. It wasn't that she didn't like her. It was just that in her vast experience whenever Allison appeared, it meant nothing good for Stacey.

She grabbed a soda out of the fridge and turned to look at Allison. She didn't say anything. Instead, she watched Allison squirm under her gaze for a few seconds. Finally, she sighed.

"What's the favor?"

"I need to crash here."

Stacey threw her hands up. "No!"

"What? Come on, Sis."

"Why do you need to crash here? I thought you were dating what's-his-name."

"Steven? Things sorta crashed and burned on that front."

"You mean his wife found out about you," Stacey scoffed.

The look on Allison's face told her that she was right. Stacey shook her head again. Allison began to plead.

"Come on, Stacey. I need a place to sleep. For like a week or two. Just until—"

"Until what? You get a new boyfriend? Another rich guy to pay your way through life?"

"Well, yeah."

"You can't keep doing this, Allison," Stacey said. "This isn't how you should plan your future."

"Save the lecture, seriously. No offense but if I did things your way, I'd be, well, here." She gestured around the kitchen.

"You are here," Stacey pointed out, leaning against the counter.

An embarrassed look crossed her sister's face. She mumbled something that Stacey couldn't hear. Stacey sighed.

"I have no room for you here. I only have two rooms, and they're both in use."

"I know. I'm not asking for a room. I'll sleep on the couch. I'll watch Tina during the day. She won't be alone."

Ah, there it was. The trump card. Her sister had a good point. With Allison there, Tina wouldn't be alone during the day. It would help her out on her days off when she looked for work, too. It would be one less thing to worry about. Allison knew it as well by the victorious look on her face.

Stacey sighed. "Fine. Two weeks."

"Great!" Allison beamed. "I promise I won't be any trouble."

"I'm sure," Stacey replied dryly.

Allison opened the fridge and pulled out a soda of her own. "This is a big help, really."

"Yeah, well, you can help with Tina and do some chores around the apartment. For as long as we have it, anyway."

"That still going on, huh?"

"Yeah." Stacey briefly thought of Charlie and shook her head. "The restaurant is closing down too."

"No shit, really?" Her sister's eyes widened. "That sucks. I'm sorry. You'll find other work though. Have you told—"

"No. I don't want to worry Tina about that yet."

"I saw her earlier. She let me in. She's getting worse, isn't she?"

"Yeah."

Pain flickered across Allison's eyes and she ran her fingers around the rim of her soda can. "That sucks. Where are you guys moving if this place gets knocked down? It's the only decent housing in the area."

"Yeah, things aren't looking that great right now from any side."

Allison sucked in a breath, looking around the kitchen. "Well, we'll figure something out. Somehow."

Stacey nodded and watched as her sister headed back into the living room. She had a strange relationship with Allison. They had been close as little girls, but life eventually lead them separate ways. Now, they rarely saw each other and usually got on each other's nerves after only a day. Allison was content with sleeping with rich men and letting them spend money on her. Stacey thought her sister could do better and should aim higher. The differences in opinion had led to strife between them.

She rubbed the temples of her forehead and went to check in on Tina. Even though Allison said she was sleeping, she still wanted to see for herself. A quick look inside the room showed Tina curled up on one side, fast asleep. The lamp was still on, and Stacey turned it off. Her grandmother stirred slightly and mumbled a name.

"Macy—"

The name was Stacey's mother. The sudden mention of her mother seemed to suck the air from her. She tried not to think of her parents. It only dredged up happier memories, which seemed to hurt her now instead of bringing her pleasure.

She tucked the covers around Tina and left the room, closing the door gently behind her. She stood in the hallway for a few seconds. In her mind, she could see Macy tucking her in at night after reading her a bed time story. Thinking back on losing her parents and grandfather and seeing her grandmother so ill constricted her heart.

She could hear Allison talking to someone on the phone in the living room. Her voice was low and hushed. Normally, Stacey would want to know who her sister was talking to this late. But she was too weary to care. Instead, she turned around and went to her own room.

She changed into her pajamas and crawled into bed. However, unlike the other night where exhaustion had won out over her worries, Stacey found herself just lying there. She stared up at the ceiling. Distantly, she could hear thumping music. It was probably the Robinsons on the first floor. They threw parties sometimes. Everyone went along with it because calling the police did nothing except piss off the Robinsons.

The events of the day replayed in her mind. More specifically, Stacey kept picturing Charlie asking her out. Why in the world had she accepted? It seemed insane to accept a date from someone working at the company that wanted them to vacate. A man like him could get any woman he wanted. Why would he want her? Not only that, but she was terrible with dates. She never knew what to say. She was unsure of herself and felt ugly during most social engagements.

Stacey groaned in her pillow. She had let herself be drawn in by the handsome man in a well-tailored suit. Maybe Charlie wouldn't call. He would realize he had had a serious lapse in judgment and wouldn't want to go out with her in the end.

I have better things to worry about than a date, Stacey reprimanded herself. Losing her job and her apartment were bigger concerns than Charlie taking her out on a date. She was going to hit the pavement hard and fast. She would find a new job and put her feelers out for another place to live.

A cute man wasn't more important than that.

With that in mind, Stacey closed her eyes and willed herself to sleep.

Chapter Six

"We close at four in the morning," the man said, "since the city changed the law about the 2 a.m. close time. That work for you?"

Not really, Stacey thought as she stared at the man. But beggars can't be choosers. She had been hoping to find a place that closed by midnight. That would give her enough time to get home and catch some sleep before she could *hopefully* work a day job. Closing at 4 a.m. would put a fly in that ointment. But Stacey didn't have any job yet.

"Yes, that's fine."

The man nodded and wrote something down. Stacey cast a wary eye around the place. It was a rundown diner with a bar shoved in one corner. It was in a bad part of town. Even the man in front of her, who hadn't bothered to tell Stacey his name, smelled of cigarettes and whiskey and it was only noon.

Stacey had taken the interview, making sure not to turn her back on any opportunity. She had been flitting from one place to the next over the past week, with different restaurants all over town calling her due to her experience. She was confident she would land one of them.

It was the office jobs that were causing problems. Without any prior experience, no one wanted to waste their time in interviewing her. Stacey sent resumes anyway, spending evenings at the library to use their computer. It had required a couple of shift changes with Amanda, so she wasn't stuck at the restaurant until too late.

The man asked her a few more run-of-the-mill questions that Stacey answered. Then he stood up.

"Well, we'll give you a call."

"Thank you for your time."

The man grunted in reply and walked away, not bothering to show her out. Stacey truly hoped it didn't come down to working there. With one last look around the dismal place, she left.

The humid afternoon air smacked her in the face as she left the diner. The heat rolled off the pavement. Stacey hated summer. It was so hot that her clothes stuck to her in a matter of moments. The sun beat down on her relentlessly. Inside the restaurant, the AC didn't work very well, but at least it offered some relief from the sweltering heat. Her own apartment's AC was garbage, too. It felt as if there was no escape from the summer sun.

As she reached the bus shelter and tried to cool off, she glanced at her phone. No call. It had been a week since Charlie had asked her out and her phone had remained silent. Part of her was relieved. That was what she wanted, wasn't it? Yet she felt a tinge of annoyance too. Perhaps she had been banking on that date more than she had led herself to believe. *Best not to think about him,* Stacey reminded herself. She had to get to work now. For whatever reason, Charlie had backed out on their date.

Work was more of the same. *Papa's Grill and Diner* featured daily specials to drum up a little extra money before the place finally closed its doors. Because of the specials, there were more customers than usual. Stacey found herself flitting around from table to table, trying to make sure everything was taken care of properly.

By the time she got home, she was wiped out. Stacey couldn't help but notice that she was feeling like that every night now. Get up, go to work, come home, and sleep. There was very little time for anything else.

This time when she came home, Allison was on the couch. Her feet were propped up on the coffee table. She hastily lowered them when she saw Stacey. Tina was sitting in the armchair near the TV. There was an infomercial playing.

"What are you guys watching?"

Tina replied, "They're selling this gizmo that is supposed to whiten your teeth with one pass."

Stacey rolled her eyes. "Sure."

"We've been making fun of it," Allison chimed up. "You get only three channels, do you know that?"

"We get whatever the little antennae can pick up," Stacey grumbled, sitting down next to her sister.

Allison faintly smelled of crushed roses. Stacey knew the scent well. Her sister wore that perfume whenever she was trying to snag a boyfriend.

"Busy day?" asked Stacey.

If Allison noticed the insult behind Stacey's words, she didn't pay attention. "Yup. Tina and I went to the deli down the street earlier."

"Oh." Stacey was surprised. "How was that?"

"Good. I ran into Jake."

Stacey scowled and didn't reply right away. Jake was Stacey's last serious boyfriend. They had been together for two years before she caught him cheating. She knew he was still in the area but mercifully, she hadn't seen him.

"How is it that I haven't seen him since we broke up but you run into him right off the bat?"

Allison shrugged. "Don't know. Just did. He asked about you."

"Of course, he did."

"So, you never think about getting back together with him?"

The question took Stacey by surprise, and she shook her head. "No way. After what he did to me? No."

"Don't blame you. He looked good though."

Stacey was going to ask why Allison thought that when Tina turned around to look at the two of them.

"Your mother used to want one of these little kits," she said out of nowhere, pointing to the silly teeth whitening kit on the screen.

Allison wrinkled her nose. "Why?"

"Oh, she was a sucker for these things," Tina said in a rare moment of clarity. "Loved buying whatever gimmick rolled through on the television."

"Never pegged Mom as the type," Stacey replied, trying to remember if she had ever seen Macy buying things like this.

Tina turned back to the TV. Whatever train of thought she had was gone already. Allison glanced over at Stacey. That was when Stacey's phone went off in her purse. Surprised, she rummaged through her bag, trying to find it.

Maybe it's a job offer, she thought hopefully. Better than that—maybe a business office was calling her for an interview. A quick glance at the screen showed her that it wasn't a number she knew. She excused herself from the living room and stepped into her bedroom.

"Hello, this is Stacey," she said primly.

"Is it really? Sounds more like a formal little robot."

Charlie. She was taken aback by the sound of his voice on the other line. Smooth and deep, it sent tingles up her spine. Stacey had given up on Charlie, thinking he wasn't going to call her. To be suddenly talking to him made her nervous.

"Hey," was all she finally said and cringed at how lame it sounded.

"Hey," Charlie echoed, and Stacey could tell that he was poking fun at her. "Sorry it took so long for me to call you."

"It's fine," Stacey replied, desperate to sound as if she hadn't thought of him once since she gave him her number. "I've been busy."

"Yeah, I had something come up and had to leave town for a week."

"Everything okay?"

"Yeah, yeah," Charlie said quickly, brushing her question off, "but I'd still like to see you if you're interested."

"I am, sure," Stacey said before she could stop herself.

"Great. When are you free?"

"I'm free this Thursday. I'm supposed to be done work at seven. Is that too late?"

"No, that's perfect. I can pick you up at eight."

"Okay." It struck her that he knew where she lived because of where he worked, but she pushed the thought out of her mind.

"Wonderful. Looking forward to seeing you, Stacey. Have a good night."

She was going to ask where they were going and what they were doing but Charlie had already hung up. She huffed, staring at the phone. He could have asked, at the very least, what she wanted to do or given some indication what he had planned.

Part of her wanted to call him back and tell him to forget it. Yet all she could do was sit down at the edge of her bed. What was it about Charlie that made her still want to see him?

A knock at the door made Stacey shove her phone under her pillow as if it was a dirty magazine. Allison stuck her head inside.

"Everything alright?"

"Yeah. I think I can handle a phone call," Stacey snapped, on edge. If Allison knew she had a date this week, she would never hear the end of it.

"Geez, calm down."

"Sorry, long day. That was Amanda from work. She wanted to go out for a drink on Thursday. You'll be home?"

"Yeah, I can be here." Allison turned to go and then stopped. "It's good you're getting out."

"You make me sound like a hermit."

"You are, sorta. You work a lot and come home and sleep." She held up her hands as if to ward off Stacey's protests. "I know why. I get it. Just saying it'd be good to get out, too."

"Thanks."

Allison gave her a small smile and left, closing Stacey's door behind her. She sighed. She didn't want to tell her sister and make a big deal out of the fact she was going on a date. But to her sister, every date was a big deal. Probably because her sister had tons of money on the line when she tried to snag a boyfriend. Stacey just wanted someone who she could share her time and have fun with.

Before Stacey knew it, it was Thursday. She was back home and in front of that dreadful mirror. She had tried on five different outfits and was growing more frustrated by the second. Not only that but she was beginning to psych herself out the longer she fussed with her appearance. The dreaded question of *'why'* was rearing its ugly head.

It was something she had to ponder and have a backup plan ready just in case. Too many times had Stacey seen guys who liked her only because of her size and nothing else, as if she wasn't a person with real emotions and feelings. Strange, she never knew if men were with her because of some kinky *big woman* fetish, or if they genuinely liked her for who she really was deep inside.

In the back of her mind, she was worried she would have a nice time with Charlie and he would expect her to sleep with him on the first date. That also happened sometimes. Guys assumed she was easy to sleep with because she would be so desperate for attention from them.

She pulled off the dress shirt she had been trying on. It didn't help things that she had no idea where they were going. On top of that, she wanted to meet Charlie outside the apartment. Both Allison and Tina were home. If Charlie knocked, she would have to fend off questions from her sister.

Finally, she settled on a navy-blue dress with a simple necklace. She grabbed her purse, slipped into her high heels and slunk into the living room. Allison was with Tina in the kitchen.

"Alright, see you later!" Stacey yelled quickly and was out the door before her sister could see her outfit or ask any questions.

Even though night had fallen, it was muggy outside. Stacey waited outside the building. In the back of her mind, she was worried that he wouldn't show up. Her anxiety was getting the better of her. She felt like a high-school girl waiting for her boyfriend to show and take her out.

But right on time, a car pulled up to the curb. Charlie got out. Stacey exhaled. At least he showed up. He looked surprised at seeing her on the street.

"Hey, I could have knocked."

"Then you'd have to meet my family," Stacey said bluntly, "so this is fine."

"What, you think they'd scare me off?"

"No, I think you'd scare them off," she retorted.

Charlie smiled at her and opened the passenger door of the car. It was a nice car, nicer than anything else she had seen in this area. It was sleek and perfectly clean which was a far cry from the cars that normally cruise around her neighborhood.

As she slid into the car, she looked at Charlie out of the corner of her eye. He was wearing a white button-up shirt. The sleeves were rolled back a little because of the heat. Something about the white shirt and the way it looked on him made her heart skip a beat. His hair wasn't slicked back, and it gave him an almost boyish charm. She could smell his cologne as she sat down.

He got in the driver's seat. "You look beautiful," he said to her.

Stacey instantly let her nerves get the better of her, and before she could stop herself, she was rambling. "Well, I wasn't sure where we were going, if it was somewhere formal or not. So, I tried to find something in the middle, if that makes sense, so no matter where we go, it'd be okay." She cut herself off before she could say anything embarrassing. She wished she could just smack herself when she rambled on like that.

But Charlie didn't seem to notice. Instead, he laughed a little. "I should have told you, shouldn't I? It's a place on the beach. But you're dressed perfectly. Promise."

Stacey smiled weakly at him, still trying to quell her nerves. Now she was worried about finding things to talk about. They would have to fill the silence in the car ride as well as dinner. That was a lot of talking. Why the hell was she so nervous? She had told this guy off in the lobby and by the tree without a problem. Now they were on a date, and she was stumbling over herself like a schoolgirl.

But Stacey didn't need to worry. Charlie seemed to sense her nervousness and took charge of the conversation. He spoke a little about where they were going to eat and then about the beach. When he started telling her how he had been at last year's summer festival, the ice broke. The summer festival at the beach was always crowded and a bit of a mess. Almost the entire city turned out for it at some point. People got drunk and rowdy. College kids would make trips out of it since they were on break. Everyone had a story about the summer festival.

By the time they arrived at the restaurant, the nervousness Stacey felt subsided. Charlie had her laughing most of the drive, and her anxiety had mostly left her. When she realized where they were eating, however, it threatened to return.

There were numerous places to dine at the beach. When Charlie had said they were going there, Stacey assumed it was at one of the middle-of-the-road eateries near the end of the beach. Now she realized he was taking her to one of the finest seafood establishments in the area.

He got out of the car and walked around to open the door. In the few seconds Stacey had to spare, she told herself to stop panicking. It was a nice place, so what? She could handle a nice place. She wasn't going to freak out.

"Have you been here before?" Charlie asked innocently as he helped her out of the car.

Stacey was distracted by his fingers gently resting on her wrist. Her skin broke out into goosebumps at the smallest touch from him. His cologne was making her head feel light. The ocean spilled out in front of them. It glittered under the moonlight. She could smell the salt from the water. There was a breeze rolling in that cooled off the summer heat.

"Stacey?"

"Sorry," she said, snapping back to the present, "No, I haven't been here. Did you really think I'd have been here?"

"Figured a beautiful woman like you would have been taken to all the best places."

Stacey chuckled as they walked toward the restaurant, "Yeah, sure. The finest delis with the best five-dollar dinner deals in town."

Charlie laughed at this. Making him laugh made her more confident. The comfortable feeling was starting to come back. Nice place or not, Stacey was at the very least with someone she liked being around. It surprised her that she enjoyed his company and he enjoyed hers.

Inside the restaurant, she was stunned into silence by how beautiful everything looked. Low lighting and the open atmosphere of the place created a relaxed feeling. The floor to ceiling windows projected the image that she was really on the beach. She assumed they'd be sitting in one of the booths near the back but instead Charlie whispered something to the host.

"This way," he said to her and gently rested his hand on her back as they walked. "We're going to sit on the balcony if that's okay."

Stacey mumbled a reply. She was still soaking in her surroundings, still wondering how she ended up on this date. Unlike the tacky joints she had seen on the beach, which seemed to love hanging fake crabs from the walls and having a Hawaiian print thrown everywhere, this place was subtle. There was no ocean theme shoved in her face. There was a small fountain in the middle of the room they passed by. Pearls rested at the bottom of the pool of water.

Around them, people were well-dressed, wearing outfits costing thousands of dollars. They were dining on food priced more than whatever Stacey made in a month as a waitress. The host opened a set of doors near the back, and they were escorted outside.

They had a fantastic view of the ocean and the diverse crowds enjoying the beach. Someone was having a picnic date. A group of kids were playing in the surf. A live band from a restaurant next door played soft music.

"Wow," Stacey breathed, "this is amazing."

"I prefer eating outside here. I like being this close to the ocean."

"You come here often?" she asked.

"Often enough. Do you drink wine?"

"Yes, but you should order it. I don't know much about wine."

Charlie turned to the host and rattled off the name of something she had never heard before. She was definitely out of her comfort zone. Stacey wasn't even sure she could see her comfort zone from where she was. Sitting in a place like this—a place she had walked by many times, envious of the people who could come here—watching someone as handsome as Charlie order wine—was an experience she never thought she would have.

Charlie turned to look out at the ocean. Stacey admired his jawline and the stubble that peppered his face. He must have felt her staring because he turned back to look at her. His eyes were a deep brown, like dark chocolate. She looked down at the menu, embarrassed that he caught her staring.

"What do you recommend here?" she asked him. "I don't know the first thing about seafood."

She felt stupid for asking him for help in ordering. It was just a restaurant after all. But Stacey wanted to find the most delicious thing on the menu. She might not get another chance to come here again. The fact she even got to come here once was enough for her. She'd rather ask for help than miss out on a delicious opportunity.

But if Charlie thought it was stupid she was asking for help, he didn't show it. Like in the car, the conversation flowed smoothly. Before she knew it, the food had arrived, and they both ate and spoke with ease. There were no awkward silences in the conversation. Stacey didn't feel as if she were stumbling over her words or having to hide details about herself.

Charlie mentioned a brother in passing but hadn't gone into any detail about him. In fact, where Stacey had spoken about her family and her living situation, Charlie hadn't really shared specifics about his. She hadn't pushed it, assuming there had been a reason for that.

The only dark cloud over the entire date was the fact that Charlie worked for the company that wanted her out of the apartment complex. She was careful to avoid it. She didn't want to bring it up, not now. It would ruin the night.

When dinner was finished, Charlie suggested walking along the beach. She agreed, eager to feel the sand in between her toes. The balcony led directly to it so after they finished, they walked down.

"Would you be offended if I took off my shoes?" she asked him.

"No, that's a good idea, actually," Charlie replied, and before she said anything else, he slipped off his shoes and socks too.

They walked along the water, allowing the waves to lap around their ankles. Stacey felt so happy that she swore she could fly up in the air if she tried hard enough. The entire night so far had felt like a fairy tale. Being swept up and taken to a nice place to eat and now walking along the beach like this felt like something she would have dreamed up late at night when she couldn't sleep.

"Been ages since I've been here," Stacey said with a little sigh. "Can't even remember the last time."

"Probably the summer festival," Charlie joked.

She smiled. "Might have been, actually."

"I was here a month ago."

"Day trip?"

"Sort of." Something crossed his face. "Wasn't enjoyable. Not compared to tonight."

A shiver snaked down Stacey's back. She felt a blush creep up her face and looked away from Charlie.

"It's getting late. I have a meeting in the morning so I should probably get you back home," he said, looking at his watch.

Stacey couldn't help but feel disappointed. Secretly, she wished the date could last for hours. She was having such a lovely time. Instead, she nodded, and they turned back toward the car.

They were almost off the beach when Charlie suddenly stopped. Stacey looked back at him curiously. He was looking up at the moon and then looked down at her. He took a step toward her. Stacey froze. He brushed a lock of her hair away from her face. The slightest touch of his fingers against her skin made each nerve feel alive and aware of how close he was to her now.

"This would be a lovely place to kiss you," Charlie said very softly, his eyes flicking to hers, "unless that would be overstepping."

Stacey's throat had gone dry. He was so close to her that she could kiss him easily. He was waiting for her to give him permission. All she could do was nod. It was enough. Charlie gently tilted her face up to his and brought his lips softly against hers. Stacey closed her eyes and returned the kiss.

It had been a long time since she had kissed a man. She couldn't remember ever kissing a man like this on a first date. Normally, she was so guarded that the date would end with a chaste kiss on the cheek and a promise to see each other soon. After a string of bad luck, Stacey hadn't ever thought she'd be kissed like this. She could hear the ocean next to them. The moonlight poured across the beach, revealing the soft waves forever making their journey up the beach before fading away in the white sand. Charlie's lips pressed against hers. It made her head spin as she closed her eyes for the kiss.

He pulled away from her after a minute or so. Stacey felt breathless as if she had just run a mile. Her heart thumped hard in her chest. Charlie gave her a little smile. His eyes crinkled when he smiled, she realized.

"Been wanting to do that all night," he murmured.

Then his hand grabbed hers. They walked back to the car together in a comfortable silence. Stacey held onto his hand the entire walk. She could feel how warm he was. During the long drive to her home, her lips tingled from his kiss.

When Charlie pulled up to the curb, he looked at her. "Want me to walk you up to the apartment?"

"Ah, no, I'm okay. My grandmother might still be awake, and I wouldn't want to startle her," Stacey said.

Charlie nodded. "I had a lovely time tonight, Stacey. I'll give you a call, okay?"

"Thank you for everything," she said, half hoping that he would kiss her again.

But he didn't. Stacey got out of the car and walked into the apartment complex. Through the grimy window, she watched him drive away into the night. Part of her was relieved that Tina and Allison were upstairs. She knew that if she had let Charlie walk her to the door, there was a big chance that she would fall into bed with him.

Trying to keep a smile off her face, she walked upstairs.

Chapter Seven

"Have a good night?" Allison asked her without looking up from her phone when Stacey opened the front door.

"Yeah, I had a nice time," she replied, trying to keep her voice neutral.

"That's good," her sister replied in a monotone voice as she typed away on her phone.

Stacey took off her shoes and asked, "How were things here?"

"Fine. Tina is asleep. I've been flirting with this friend of Steven's, and I think he is going to want to see me tomorrow."

"Gosh, I'm so happy for you," Stacey deadpanned.

Allison finally looked up and rolled her eyes. "No lecture, please. Also, you wore that to hang out with Amanda? Trying to get laid or something?"

"Why are you so crass all the time?"

She shrugged. "Is it crass or is it just the truth?"

"Crass. Anyway, I'm tired and going to bed. Good luck with your flirting."

Allison arched a brow. "Definitely trying to get laid then. No luck. Well, next time, Sis."

Stacey ignored her and walked to her room. She was glad she hadn't told Allison about the date. In her room, she stripped off her dress and hopped in the shower. She smelled like the beach and wanted to get the sand off her feet.

In the shower, Stacey made the water as hot as she could tolerate and stood underneath the spray. It pounded against her skin. She closed her eyes and let it wash over her.

Her mind drifted back to Charlie. She couldn't believe how hard she had fallen for him on the first date. She had wanted more than just a simple kiss. Stacey had wanted his hands on her body and his lips across her skin. Just thinking about him like that made her body ache.

Surely, he had enjoyed himself too. She hated to think that she wasn't going to hear from him again. She had felt a true connection with him. Their conversations had gone well. Dinner had been lovely. The walk on the beach had been perfect.

Stacey finished her shower and dried off. She changed into pajamas and curled up in bed. This time, she had trouble falling asleep because she couldn't stop thinking of Charlie taking her in the worst way, or the best way.

<<◇>>

The weekend was a blur of work and sleep. Stacey managed to fit in a couple more interviews as well. They were all for restaurants. She had had no luck in finding an interview for an office job yet.

During the long hours of working at the practically empty restaurant, Stacey had more time than she would have liked to think about Charlie. She hadn't heard from him since their dinner and was trying not to think negatively about it. Didn't everyone wait a few days to reach out after a date now? Stacey knew she sorely lacked information on what the dating scene was like but was too embarrassed to ask anyone for advice.

Stacey had ended up with Monday off after a last-minute schedule shift with Maria. Allison had already made plans to take Tina out for the day, leaving Stacey home alone for the first time in what seemed like ages.

"Are you sure you want to take her out?" Stacey asked her sister as they got ready to leave.

"Yes. Will you calm down? We're just going to the beach."

"You aren't—you aren't meeting some guys there are you?"

Allison scowled, and Stacey knew she had gone a little too far. Her sister was a lot of things, but she had never done anything to disrespect their grandmother.

"Really, Stacey? You're going to be a bitch right now?"

"No, sorry. I'm sorry. I'm glad you're spending time with her. Maybe I should—"

"You're not coming with us," Allison said shortly, still irritated with her. "I don't know. Do something fun. We'll be back tonight."

With that, she turned away to help Tina down the stairs. Stacey watched them go and sat down on the couch. Time seemed to stretch out in front of her. It made the most sense to go to the library and send more resumes to different places. She probably would have been able to go with Allison and her grandmother if she hadn't suggested her sister had an ulterior motive for the outing.

Stacey sighed and went to grab her things. Going to the library and applying for work on her day off wasn't her idea of fun. But what else was she going to do? If she sat around and watched TV, she'd be dwelling on how she could be doing something productive.

There was a knock on the door. *Allison probably forgot her keys,* Stacey thought as she went to open the door. She opened it without checking through the peephole. So, when she saw Charlie there, she blinked in surprise.

"Hey. Sorry for popping by like this. I wasn't sure if you'd be home or not. Are you busy?"

Stacey was still thrown off by Charlie appearing at her door. He was dressed for work, in a suit and tie, reminding her yet again of just what he did for a living.

Even so, her heart thumped against her chest at seeing him.

"No. I ended up having the day off. Are you, uh, are you here because of the apartment situation?"

Charlie shook his head, "Not exactly. I was here for work and thought I'd come by and see you."

Stacey smiled, "Want to come in? My sister and grandmother went to the beach."

She moved aside to allow Charlie to enter. He looked around the living room. For a few moments, Stacey tensed. She realized that someone who could afford to eat where they had for dinner the other night probably thought her place looked like a shit hole. But if Charlie thought it was a dismal little place, it didn't reflect on his face.

Instead he turned to look at her. "You didn't go with them?"

"I sorta pissed off my sister," she replied, feeling bashful. "I wasn't exactly invited. Do you want anything to drink?"

"Water is fine," he said and followed her into the kitchen. "Can't imagine you pissing anyone off."

"My sister and I have a messy sort of relationship. You said you have a brother, right? Do you two get along?" She handed him a bottle of water, secretly glad that Allison had bought some the other day. She doubted Charlie had meant tap water when he had asked.

Her hunch about his sibling was correct when he replied with, "No. Not really."

"That's rough."

"What can you do, right?"

"Is he older?"

"No, younger. Maybe that's why we don't get along. Older siblings are always in charge of things. The younger ones get to run around wild and free."

Stacey thought of Allison and found herself nodding her head in agreement. "Yeah, and you never know when they are going to get serious and grow up."

"Well, if she is anything like you, then I'm sure she will figure things out."

Silence fell between them. She hadn't missed the fact that she was home alone with Charlie. He had to have noticed that as well? But he was working. He wouldn't act on anything he was feeling during his workday, would he?

Stacey crossed her arms self-consciously. "You said you were here for work?"

"Yeah. Talking to a couple of people."

"People who want to take the deal?" she pressed and then shook her head. "Sorry. I shouldn't ask about your work."

Charlie took a step toward her. "I've wanted to call you and see if you would go out again. But, you know, I get it. With everything going on, I mean. If you don't want to see me anymore."

She should tell him that she shouldn't. It was wrong, wasn't it, to date a man working so hard to evict all these families from their homes? But already her mind was attempting to justify it. It wasn't like he owned the company or oversaw the project. Everyone had to pay their bills. Everyone had to scrape by. Wouldn't she do the same in his position?

"I want to see you again," she heard herself say. "I'm glad you're here."

A smile broke out across Charlie's face. He seemed relieved at the fact that Stacey wanted to see him again. Before she could stop herself, she crossed the short distance between them and pressed her lips against his.

Charlie's hands snaked up her back as he returned the kiss. His fingers went to her hair, sending shivers down her back. Her own hands wrapped around his waist. Any fears or concerns she had about making the first move faded. With Charlie, it felt natural to be wrapping her arms around him. It felt right to have his lips on hers. Had it only been a weekend since she had seen him? Somehow, the distance felt a lot longer. It felt as if she had been walking ages to get to him.

The kisses grew deeper. Every nerve in Stacey's body felt awake and alive, yearning for more from Charlie. His fingers trailed down her neck, and his lips followed. She could feel her heart beating hard as he pressed himself against her.

"Come with me," she whispered and laced her fingers through his.

Chapter Eight

Stacey led him to her bedroom. Everything felt as if they were moving in slow motion. She swore she was in a dream as she turned around to face him. His lips found hers again.

There was no other conversation. None was needed. They were home alone and in her room. They both knew exactly what they wanted from each other. All the insecurities that Stacey usually felt when she was going to have sex with a guy faded to the background. Her mind was buzzing with an energy focused solely on Charlie, to touch him.

They teased each other as they took their clothes off, tossing them in a heap. Soon, they were both on her bed, very naked. He dragged his lips across her neck. She trailed her fingers across his back as he brought his lips back down on hers. She could feel how stiff he was against her thighs. The only thing separating them was his boxers. Everything else had been stripped away.

Charlie brought his lips to her nipples and flicked his tongue across them. Stacey closed her eyes and marveled at how that small touch could make pleasure radiate through her body.

He played with her breasts, squeezing them and sucking on her nipples before moving down lower. He left kisses along her belly and down her thighs as he opened her legs. Before Stacey could say anything, Charlie's tongue ran down her pussy.

She gasped in surprise. It had been so long since anyone had done that. Jake had always whined if she had asked to the point where she had stopped asking. But there was no hesitation on Charlie's end. His tongue probed her wetness gently, sending shivers throughout Stacey's body.

His tongue found her clit, and he flicked his tongue against it. She arched her hips slightly and her toes curled in delight. Charlie took this as a sign to keep going. He began to alternate between licking her clit and running his tongue down the length of her wetness.

The pleasure was overwhelming. Stacey had her eyes squeezed shut as Charlie brought her close to climax. She couldn't stop herself. As he brought his lips to her clit, she lost it. Her hips buckled, and her orgasm rolled through her. Her moans filled the air as Charlie worked his tongue into her pussy, letting her orgasm take her over.

As she lay there, breathless, Charlie brought himself up from between her thighs. He kissed her passionately. She could taste herself on his mouth, and it brought a thrill to her. Her hands fumbled with his boxers. She wanted them off. She wanted his cock inside of her, and she wanted it now.

With his boxers thrown to the floor, she pressed herself against him. Charlie's fingers were in her hair as he began to enter her. He was thick, and it took a little wiggling around on Stacey's part to get his cock fully inside of her.

Once he was in, however, he let out a soft moan. Something about hearing Charlie utter those noises made Stacey crazy. She dug her nails into his back and began to move her hips against him.

Charlie took the hint. He began to move inside of her. At first, he went slowly. There was a grin on his face as he watched her wiggle underneath him, wanting more.

"Don't tease me," she whispered.

"Why?" he replied quietly, leaning down to kiss her. "You don't like being teased?"

"No, not by you." She smiled against his skin as he moved deeper inside of her.

Charlie laughed in her ear—it was low and throaty, filled with desire, "Maybe that's why I want to tease you."

Their lips found each other again, and this time he began to move harder. His thrusts became more urgent as they clung to each other. Stacey could hear Charlie moaning, and she timed her own hip thrusts to go against his movements.

The only thing she could focus on was how his cock felt inside of her. She was breathless. Their bodies were slick with sweat as they fucked. Every noise Charlie made turned her on more. Each kiss they had was enough to drive her wild. The sensation of being filled by him was more than she could take.

When she came again, so did Charlie. They came together, holding each other as if they were each other's life raft.

As their orgasms subsided, Charlie rolled off her. Together, they lay there, trying to catch their breath. After climaxing two times, Stacey felt exhausted. She had never had an orgasm with Jake. He had always finished quickly and then fell asleep. She didn't know her body could respond with someone like it just had with Charlie.

Sleepily, she turned to look at him. He looked at her and smiled.

"Probably shouldn't have done that while I was working," he joked.

Stacey smiled. "Ah, well. Live a little."

He leaned over to her. His lips grazed hers. Stacey responded by pressing her lips against his. They kissed like this for a few minutes until he pressed his forehead against hers.

"I should go. But I'll call you."

"Okay," she said, smiling a little. "Thanks for stopping by."

"Thanks for having me," he replied.

Stacey watched him dress. She admired the way his body looked. It was clear he worked out religiously. His muscles looked amazing even in the low light of her room. His fingers deftly did up the buttons on his dress shirt. He ran his fingers through his hair, trying to flatten it from where Stacey had mussed it up.

She watched him from her bed, still lying there naked. Her limbs felt as if they weighed a thousand pounds each. Even her eyelids were heavy. When Charlie finished getting dressed, he leaned over and gave her one last kiss.

"I'll see myself out," he laughed gently.

Stacey murmured something in reply. She heard him leave the room as she curled up on her side, lazily dragging her blanket over her naked body. The front door closed. Before she could think of anything else, she fell asleep, feeling content for the first time in ages.

Chapter Nine

"Where are you going?" Stacey asked Allison who had been hogging the bathroom for over an hour.

Currently, her sister was leaning over the counter. She had a mascara brush in her hand and was opening and closing her mouth like a fish as she tried to apply it. She stopped what she was doing and looked over at Stacey.

"I have a date tonight." Allison's tone was frosty.

Stacey sighed. "Are you still upset about my remark from the other day?"

"The one where you implied I was only spending time with our grandmother because I had some ulterior motive to pick up a man?"

"I said I was sorry."

It was true. When Stacey got home late from work last night, Allison was still awake. For once, her sister had her nose in a book although the cover looked as if it was one of those cheesy pulp novels that she loved so much for some reason. She hadn't looked up when Stacey had gotten home.

Stacey had apologized there on the spot. She didn't want to be in the cramped apartment with her sister and not be on speaking terms. Allison was family, after all, frustrating or not. She had grunted in reply which hadn't exactly left Stacey feeling confident. Allison could hold a grudge over both big and little things.

Clearly, she wasn't over it yet. She had turned back to the mirror and finished applying the mascara. Stacey looked her over. She was wearing a sleek black dress that had a hint of glitter on the hem and sleeves. It brought out the darkness of her skin and accentuated her hips. She looked beautiful. Whatever man she had snagged for this date would no doubt be sucked in.

Allison picked up a tube of lipstick. From here, Stacey could see it was a dark red.

"Good shade," she remarked.

Allison didn't bother to look over at her. "Of course, it is. Brings out my eyes."

"Well, good luck with your date. Can you tell me where you're going at least? In case something happens."

"What could happen? You think I have shitty judgment or something?"

"No, Allison. You're my sister. Just want to make sure you are safe. It has nothing to do with your dating options or anything," Stacey replied, feeling tired from dealing with Allison.

Her sister paused and then replied, "That banquet downtown. Hodge's Benefit."

Stacey's eyes widened, "You're going to *that*?"

Even though Allison was still irritated with her, the chance to gloat was too much for her to resist. She put down the lipstick and looked over at her. A small smile crossed her face.

"That guy I mentioned I was texting? The friend of my ex? Well, he invited me to it."

"That's one of the biggest events of the entire year."

"I know," Allison replied primly.

Stacey couldn't believe it. Hodge's Banquet was where the richest of the rich went once a year. The event was technically created to raise money for a charity to help with education, but over the years, the focus shifted less on the charity and more toward the event itself so the rich could showboat.

It always garnered massive media attention in the city. Celebrities had begun to attend as well over the years. Tickets were almost impossible to get. If Allison was going, then whomever she was dating must be a big shot.

"Who is this guy, anyway?"

"His name is Jacob Benson. Works in oil."

"Never heard of him. Not like that matters. I don't know anyone with more than twenty dollars at one time," Stacey joked.

Allison looked serious for a moment and said, "Listen, I know you think what I do is sort of silly. Snagging rich guys and—"

"Living off them?"

"I'll let that slide," Allison replied dryly, "only because I'm in a good mood. But Jacob is a high roller. I mean, he has billions to his name. He's single too. Do you get what I'm saying?"

"You're going to try to succeed where all other women have failed and try to snag a marriage out of him?" Stacey shook her head, "Won't ever work."

"And why not?"

"That guy probably already knows that you have that in mind. If he is worth billions of dollars, then he has seen every sort of woman try to win his heart. He's probably going into this date knowing you want to marry him. I wouldn't get your hopes up."

The words seemed to go in one ear and out another with her sister because she had turned back to the mirror, clearly tuning Stacey out.

"We'll see," she finally said, looking up at her.

"Well, have a good time."

Stacey left her sister alone in the bathroom. Tina was coming down the hallway.

"Allison still here?" she asked her.

"Yeah, she's getting ready."

Tina clicked her tongue against the roof of her mouth. "Wasting her time, that girl. Never understood why she is constantly trying to marry rich."

"Well, just let her do her thing. We aren't going to change her mind now, are we? Would you like something to drink?" Stacey asked her grandmother, lacing her arm through hers.

"Hot milk would be lovely."

"Come on then."

She led Tina to the small dining room table and then went to heat up some milk for her. Allison appeared a few minutes later. She really did look stunning. With a pang in her chest, Stacey looked away. She hated comparing herself to her sister, but how could she not? Where Allison was thin and currently looked as if she had stepped out of the pages of a glossy magazine, Stacey felt plain and gross standing there.

"You look beautiful," Tina spoke first, getting up to give Allison a big hug, "And I hope you have a wonderful time."

"Thanks. I'm sure I will," she said with a bright smile. "He's sending a car for me so I should head downstairs."

Stacey bit her tongue. She wanted to ask what sort of billionaire couldn't pick up his date himself but she knew it would only piss her sister off more. Allison turned to look at her, awaiting a compliment.

"You look gorgeous. If he isn't smart enough to fall head over heels for you, then you don't need him," Stacey said automatically.

Allison beamed. This was how it had always been, she thought somewhat bitterly. Her sister got the dates with the gorgeous guys. As a teenager, it was the popular kids in school. Stacey could recall plenty of times where Allison had come down the stairs dressed to the nines for a date. Stacey would prattle off compliments to her and watch her leave. She had always secretly been upset.

Now, it still stung. Not only because Allison was going off to the biggest event of the year looking so beautiful, but also because since Stacey had slept with Charlie, she hadn't heard from him.

As she watched her sister leave, she couldn't help but wonder if she had made a serious mistake with Charlie. Allison constantly tried to snag a rich husband. Coming from a poor background, she craved the sort of life they had dreamed about as little girls. Stacey didn't agree with how her sister was doing things, but she always seemed to know how to handle men.

On the opposite side of that, Stacey felt as if she bumbled her way through relationships. Her last serious relationship, with Jake, had blown up in her face. She had been confident in that one. Sure, he hadn't been perfect, but she had been willing to overlook that to be with him. She had a long trail of broken relationships behind her. Jake had merely been the only one that felt like it might really stick.

Now she had jumped into bed with Charlie because she felt so connected to him. It had been a passion that felt almost impossible to fend off. As she watched Allison close the front door behind her, heading off into the night, Stacey wondered what Charlie was doing at this very moment. No doubt her sister would have handled it better than she had. Her sister seemed to understand men. She had an innate ability to wrap them around her finger and get what she wanted. Stacey just seemed to bungle it up at every chance.

"Dear?" Tina's voice snapped her out of her thoughts.

Stacey shook her head. "Sorry. Warm milk. I forgot."

She went back to the kitchen, vowing to try not to think of Allison or Charlie that night.

Chapter Ten

"I accepted it," Stacey said to Amanda the next day at the restaurant, "It's a nicer place than here, and it's something, at least."

Amanda nodded, pouring herself what was probably her fourth cup of coffee. "Sounds good. You said they close at midnight? I haven't actually ever been there."

That morning, Stacey had gotten a job offer at a diner down the street from where she currently worked. It was a fifties-themed place that seemed to bring in steady clients. When she interviewed there last week, they actually had a lunch rush. She couldn't recall the last time she had handled a rush of any sort. They closed at midnight, which meant she could still swing a second day job. She was starting to lose hope at ever finding an office job.

"Yup. So, I have that covered at least."

"What about the apartment situation?"

"Still bad. They're offering us money to vacate. Most of us are banding together, but I think a couple of people are planning on taking the money to go and risk finding a new place to live."

"That area you live in is the last place in this entire city that is affordable and not in a shitty section of the city. If my parents weren't helping me out with college, I'd probably move."

"Where would you go?" Stacey asked curiously.

Amanda took a sip of her coffee. "No idea. Guess we are both stuck here, right?"

"Guess so."

"Well, I'm sure you'll figure it out. Even after this place closes down, we'll keep in touch. I'll keep my ear to the ground for anything about a solid place to move into."

"Thanks," Stacey replied and meant it.

Amanda headed out to deal with the couple of customers they had. For the thousandth time that day, Stacey peeked out of the kitchen to see if Charlie was there. It was silly and made her feel like a schoolgirl. He had shown up there once. If he was avoiding her, would he show up there again?

There was no change inside the diner. Stacey slumped against the wall and tried not to berate herself. Why had she gotten so hung up on this guy so quickly? It was so stupid of her. Better to forget the entire thing.

William stuck his head in. "I have the paper here. I was going to throw it out but wanted to see if you'd like a look first?"

"Yeah, sure," Stacey mumbled, "I'll take it."

She took it from him, thinking she could give it to Tina that night to read. William shot her a quick smile and walked away. He had a little jaunt in his step lately. Of course, he did. He was finally going to turn a profit on this place by selling it.

Stacey went to the break room and shoved the newspaper in her purse. She yawned. She had stayed up too late last night, waiting for Allison to get home. She had fallen asleep before she heard her sister come in. By the time she got up for work, however, Allison was fast asleep on the couch in some baggy t-shirt and sweatpants.

At least I have another job waiting, she told herself firmly. That was one goal accomplished. She just had to figure out how she was going to afford everything plus moving.

Stacey told herself to stop dwelling and get to work. She would take things as they came and forget about Charlie as much as she could.

When she got home that evening, Tina was watching TV. She had a pair of knitting needles in her lap which looked as if they hadn't been touched at all. Stacey could hear Allison in the kitchen heating something up in the microwave.

"Hello, dear. How was your day?"

"It was good." For a moment, she considered telling her grandmother about her new job but realized she would then have to explain that her current place of employment was closing.

"That you, Stacey?" Allison called from the kitchen.

"Yup. Hey, how did it go last night?" she asked as she walked over to her.

Her sister looked over her shoulder. "You wouldn't believe it even if I tried to explain it. It was crazy. It was filled with the most gorgeous people I have ever seen in my life! Honestly, I felt a little out of my element. My dress wasn't designer or anything, but I made it work, you know? My charm saw me through."

"Right," Stacey said slowly, "I meant how was Jacob? Did you two get along? Were you nervous?"

"I'm never nervous," Allison boasted.

Stacey stopped herself from rolling her eyes. While she was glad her sister apparently had a nice time, she could tell this was going to make her even more insufferable than normal.

"But no, he was nice. I'm convinced he's hooked on me. He is definitely going to want to see me again. I had his friends eating out of the palm of my hand. And look!" She turned around and stuck her hand out toward Stacey.

On her wrist dangled a tennis bracelet. It was brimming with diamonds. Allison studied Stacey's face very carefully. Even though Stacey knew she should be happy for her sister, she couldn't help but want to snatch the item off her wrist. Why keep such a trinket? If they pawned that thing, they wouldn't have to worry about money for ages.

"Pretty," was all she could muster up the strength to say.

Allison seemed disappointed by this and yanked her arm away. "Jacob gave this to me. Do you know how much this thing probably cost him?"

"Enough for us to pay rent somewhere nice for probably six months in advance," Stacey retorted.

Allison scowled. "Don't."

"Don't what?"

"Don't lecture me. I knew I shouldn't have shown you."

"Yet you still did," Stacey said, feeling the irritation swoop over her swiftly. "You still showed me a bracelet that could fix almost all of our problems."

"No, *your* problems," Allison snapped back. "Your problems, not mine, Stacey. It isn't my fault you're broke."

"Are you fucking serious right now? You're staying with me *because you have no place to live*. Because you technically never have anywhere to live. You flit around from one rich guy to the other, unable to lock any of them down to get the money you want!"

Allison spun around as the microwave beeped. The frozen dinner stunk up the kitchen, which only seemed to remind her of the situation. She wrinkled her nose.

"Oh, excuse me, Stacey. Sorry that I am trying to get out of my shitty situation. All you do is work at some dead-end job without ever trying to better yourself or move onto something new!"

"Better myself? That's rich coming from you! How exactly do you better yourself? Spread your legs wider each time?"

Allison's face blushed. It spread across her features. Stacey was furious as well. She wished she could slap her sister but instead just took a step back. It had been a long time since the two of them fought, mostly because they avoided seeing each other for this very reason.

"You're just jealous," Allison hissed through clenched teeth. "That's all it has ever been with you."

"What the fuck would I be jealous about? At least I have a place to live."

"You're jealous because I have confidence and people flock to me. You never had that, Stacey. You were always in the background, seething with jealousy over what I brought to the table."

Stacey shook her head although she couldn't think of anything to say back. To be honest, it was the truth. She had always been jealous of her sister. Her sister had always gotten the attention and the boys. Stacey had always felt fat and ugly compared to her.

Even if it did hit close to home, there was no way she was going to let her sister know that. Allison had crossed her arms. The pinkish hue that had spread out across her face contrasted with her dark skin. Even now she looked pretty. Stacey was sure she looked like a mess compared to her sister.

"I was nice enough to let you stay here when your boyfriend decided to stay with his *wife,* and this is how you treat me?"

"So what, you going to kick me out?" Allison stuck her chin out as if daring her. "I have nowhere to go."

"That isn't my problem," Stacey said, raising her voice again. "It isn't my fault—"

"Girls! Enough!"

They both looked over to see that Tina had wandered into the kitchen. Her face, normally serene, looked taut and irritated at the sight of the two sisters fighting. Instantly, Stacey felt ashamed. She didn't want to fight with Allison and stress out her grandmother.

"Enough of this," Tina repeated, "I can hear you out in the living room. This bickering doesn't suit either one of you." She looked at Allison. "Is this true? You have nowhere to go?"

Allison looked embarrassed at having her lie exposed. She looked down at the floor and mumbled something.

Tina shook her head, "Nowhere to live. You should be treating your sister with more respect than that if she is letting you stay here, Allison. As for you," she looked over at Stacey, "you shouldn't speak to your sister like that. Neither of you should be treating each other so disrespectfully. In this house, we only love each other, do you understand me?"

"Yes," the two women said in unison as if they were little girls being chastised.

"I'm going to bed. No more fighting, understand?"

The girls agreed again and watched Tina go. Stacey waited until she heard the bedroom door close before she exhaled. Allison yanked her frozen dinner out of the microwave violently, still clearly simmering with irritation over the fight.

Stacey trailed after her. She wanted to say something but didn't know what. Somehow, they always ended up fighting like this. She wasn't sure if they'd ever smooth things over. Both had their pride. Stacey would never admit she was jealous of Allison, and she would never tell her sister what she really thought about their relationship.

Trying to find a topic of conversation, Stacey pulled out the newspaper that William had given to her earlier and plopped it on the table.

"If you want something to read," she said with a small shrug.

Allison's eyes lit up, "Hey, I wonder if any photos of me are in here?"

Of course, Stacey thought, the mere idea that Allison could find a photo of herself in the paper was enough to let her forget their fight. Instead of making a catty remark, she just sat down.

"You should look."

Allison was already opening the paper. The front page was about the event. There was a photo of two men heading into the banquet hall. From where she stood, Stacey couldn't make out their faces. Allison looked disinterested and opened the paper up, eager to find more of the story.

After a few minutes, her sister found the full-page coverage of the event. Her eyes scanned the images, but she pouted.

"Jacob is in here but not me."

"Let me see," Stacey said, curious to see the billionaire that her own sister was seeing.

She slid the paper over to her and Stacey studied the man. The newspaper photo was grainy, so it was hard to make him out. He was turned to the left speaking to someone and had a champagne flute in his hand. From there, he looked very dignified, but it was impossible to make out other details.

"He's probably talking to me too," Allison whined, "but they cropped me out because I'm a nobody."

"Sorry about that," Stacey said although she didn't see why Allison was so upset—she still got to go, didn't she?

She closed the newspaper, and for the first time, Stacey saw the image of the front page. For a few seconds, she just stared at it. Her sister must have noticed because she stopped eating.

"Nice looking, huh?"

Stacey didn't reply.

Oblivious, Allison kept going. "I wouldn't find him too attractive though. Maybe at first glance, I was like 'oh wow, cute,' but not after."

Stacey found her voice. "After what?"

Her sister beamed again. She always looked pleased to be the first one to break some gossip to her first. In this case, Stacey's chest tightened even more as she waited to hear what Allison had to say.

"That guy is the owner of the company trying to kick us all out. He's like, a total billionaire. Charlie Albert. He owns the investment and construction company that is trying to rebuild this section of the city." She tapped his face in the picture with her index finger. "I wanted to tell him off, but you know. It wouldn't have been classy at an event like that."

For a few seconds, Stacey felt as if she couldn't breathe. All she could do was stare at Charlie's photo in the newspaper. The caption underneath the photo backed up what her sister had just told her.

Charlie didn't just work at Lexington and Albert Construction. He owned the company. He owned all of it. He was a billionaire, and he was the *bad guy* trying to take over the complex, trying to take their home.

Chapter Eleven

"Are you okay?" Allison asked, peering closely at Stacey. "You look like you're going to barf."

"I just—just don't feel well all of a sudden," Stacey replied lamely.

Her sister leaned across the table and put the back of her hand against Stacey's forehead and frowned. "You feel clammy. You should get to bed before you get sick or something. I don't want to catch anything."

Stacey couldn't even be annoyed by her sister thinking only of herself again. Instead, she merely nodded and stood up. She felt extremely dizzy as the newspaper stared back up at her. Charlie, posing with what was probably another billionaire, hadn't magically vanished or changed to someone else. It was really him.

"I'm gonna take this," Stacey said and crumpled it in her hands before Allison even answered. "Goodnight."

"Yeah, take it. I'm not in it, so I don't care. Listen, get some sleep, okay?"

Stacey mumbled something and headed toward her room. She felt cold all over as if she had been dunked in a tank of ice water or something. She managed to get inside her room and shut the door before the feeling overwhelmed her again. She leaned against the door and looked at the newspaper.

Charlie was the owner of the company that was responsible for trying to kick everyone out. She had been trying to justify dating him when she thought he just worked there. *He owned it*. He owned the company that wanted them out! He wanted to knock this place down and rebuild it for more of his rich friends.

Why hadn't she noticed this before? How stupid was she that she dated—no, fucked—the man who was a billionaire owner of a company that was causing her nothing but strife? Standing there, Stacey couldn't help but feel like an idiot. She opened the newspaper and scanned the article.

For the most part, it was only about the banquet. It detailed the history of the event and how popular it was. Near the end of the article was a small blurb about the sort of business people who turn up. Charlie was mentioned as a *dashing bachelor worth billions with his construction, media, and other ventures through his investment firm.*

Furiously, Stacey crumpled up the newspaper and threw it at the wall. It bounced pitifully and landed on the floor. It wasn't as if she could even corner Charlie and demand to know why he hadn't told her. She hadn't heard from him since they slept together. Now she knew why. He was probably one of those guys that liked the chase. He probably got a kick out of fucking someone he was trying to kick out of their own home.

Tears sprung to her eyes. Stacey had been so sure that this time was different. Everything with Charlie had felt natural. But it had all been a lie. Someone like that was fantastic with people. He probably had her pegged from the start. She had fallen right for it. Now all she had was the relief that she hadn't told anyone about the date or the fact she had sex with him. Her shame would remain her own.

Stacey curled up in bed and tried to push Charlie out of her mind. Yet it seemed impossible. Her night was spent in a fretful mood.

Even though Stacey had strived to forget Charlie, it proved to be impossible. The more she swore she wouldn't think about him, the more he seemed to pop up into her mind.

She should have been expecting it then when Charlie showed up to the restaurant a few days after she had discovered the truth. It was almost as if Stacey had summoned him by mere thought. One second, the restaurant had a few families coming in for dinner. The next, Charlie stood in the doorway as if conjured up by will.

Stacey had been taking drink orders from a table when she saw him out of the corner of her eye. Her throat went dry. As usual, she and Amanda had been splitting the hostess duties since William wasn't going to hire a new one.

Quickly, she scribbled down the drink orders and ran off to the kitchen. Amanda was back there, flirting with Brad. She had always had a crush on the gruff cook but had put off trying to score with him because they worked together. As Stacey watched Amanda lean over to him and twirl her hair, she assumed that was now out the window.

"Amanda!"

She looked up and shot Brad a smile before walking over to her. "One of my tables complaining?"

"No, but they will be if you keep holding up our one cook," Stacey said pointedly.

Amanda looked a little embarrassed but brushed it off. "What is it?"

"Remember that guy you thought had a cute butt? The one talking to me before?"

"Yes. Why, is he here?"

"Yeah, but I need you to seat him for me. Please? In your section. Please!" she pleaded.

"Sure, sure, relax. Is he bothering you? Want me to deal with him?"

The idea of Amanda 'dealing' with anyone was comical, but Stacey was too panicked to even laugh.

Instead, she shook her head. "No, no, I just don't want to talk to him."

"Alright, I'll handle it."

Stacey watched her leave and leaned against the wall. Brad had turned his attention back to his actual job of cooking. Each second Amanda spent out there felt like hours to Stacey. How long did it take to seat him?

After a minute that felt like an hour, Amanda stuck her head into the kitchen. "Hey, he wants to see you. I tried to tell him you went on break but he called my bluff."

"What did you say?"

"I said you didn't want to see him."

Stacey went over to her, flustered. "You said what?"

"I said you didn't want to see him. Don't look at me like that! You don't!"

"I'm working right now. I can't talk to him."

Amanda shrugged. "Well, he's waiting for you. I can tell him to sit down and eat. I don't think he's going to leave."

"I'll just take my break now," Stacey grumbled. "Thanks, Amanda."

She didn't want to talk to Charlie. What was there to say? Whatever he had come to tell her, she wasn't interested. Steeling herself, she went out to the dining area. He was waiting by the front door still. He had his phone out and was typing away. *Probably about the city. How to knock it down. Closing a deal worth millions.* The thought fueled her toward him. He must have sensed her because he looked up.

Stacey faltered only a little at the sight of him. He was so gorgeous just standing there. She could recall the way his skin had felt against hers and how he sounded when he was moaning in pleasure. The thought threatened to make her blush, so she fixed her gaze above his head, so she didn't have to look directly at him.

"Hey, sorry to bother you while you're working," he said and then frowned. "Uh, your friend? She said that you didn't want to see me."

"Why are you here?" Stacey snapped and crossed her arms as if to ward him off.

Charlie's confusion was clear on his face for a few seconds before he cleared his throat. "I'm sorry I didn't get back to you sooner. If you're upset about that, I completely understand—"

"Let's talk outside, okay?" Stacey said, not wanting to tell him off in front of the entire restaurant.

He followed her outside. She walked to the side of the building. It was littered with cigarette butts. Maria snuck out there throughout the day for smoke breaks and never bothered to clean up. If it bothered Charlie, it didn't show on his face.

He kept on with what he had been saying before. "I'm sorry it took me so long to get back to you. I had to go out of town again and just got back. No excuse, I know. I should have called—"

"Stop. Just stop, please. Charlie, I have no interest in seeing you again."

He looked surprised and blinked a couple of times. He probably wasn't used to getting dumped. Why would he be? He probably swept people off their feet at the mere mention of his money.

"Why?"

"I saw the paper the other day. With you on the cover. I know who you are."

"Shit, Stacey, let me explain."

"No." She held up her hand. "No, I don't want to hear it. You know I can't see you anymore, right? Not only did you lie about who you were but you own the company that is trying to fuck me over royally."

"That isn't true. If you could let me explain—"

"Explain what? Explain it to me then. Explain to me how the only place I am going to be able to afford is the ghetto. Moving my grandmother into the slums all because people like you think it's nothing to knock down sections of town and rebuild it for the rich and famous. You can't explain to me what I already know, Charlie."

"We're just improving it, Stacey. It's a solid piece of the city. It just needs improving."

"And by 'improving' you mean making sure everyone that isn't worth a lot of money ships out, right?"

Charlie was shaking his head. "No. That isn't true. We are offering money for your complex to vacate—"

"Yeah, great. So now I have some money to move into the slums. I'm paying more to live there, by the way, than I am here. So, I'm paying more for a worse area. What a great trade off."

Charlie spoke again, but she barely heard it. It sounded like a sales pitch. He was on autopilot, she realized. Of course, he was. Hadn't he been pitching this to plenty of people already? Anyone who had the same concerns that she had may have spoken to Charlie already. The human side of him that had endeared Stacey had faded and was replaced by the businessman.

"I don't care," she said bluntly.

He fell silent. Not for the first time tonight, he looked surprised. No one probably spoke to him this way.

"Why did you waste my time?" Stacey asked him. "Asking me out and sleeping with me. You lied about who you were. You knew it wasn't going to work out. You knew I would eventually find out who you were."

Charlie took a step toward her. Even though she wanted to take a step back, Stacey felt rooted to the spot. He looked genuinely upset now. When he looked at her with those puppy dog eyes, part of her wanted to lean forward and press her lips against his. *Get your shit together*, she told herself roughly.

"I wanted to tell you. I just didn't know how to bring it up."

"What about as soon as we met? When I told you off in the lobby, you should have said something then. Or when you helped Kevin out of the tree. You didn't tell me then either."

"I know. I didn't think that I would like you so much, Stacey. I didn't think I'd feel so connected to you. I was afraid that once you knew who I was and what I was doing, I'd lose you," Charlie said, pleading with her.

He reached out for her arm but she took a step away from him, trying to put more space in between them. Stacey was worried that if he managed to touch her, she would crumble. Some part of her felt weak to his words. He was right, wasn't he? She wouldn't have wanted to see him again if she had known who he was. Things would have been different.

But as soon as she thought it, she pushed the thought out of her mind. It was still wrong. Charlie should have been honest with her.

"You should have told me upfront. I don't know what would have happened. But now I know for sure I can't see you again," she said, hoping she sounded confident in her choice.

"You're telling me you would have gone out with me if you knew who I was? You know you wouldn't have. I've—" His voice caught for a moment before he cleared it. "I've never had someone not know who I am before. And I wanted to see you."

Her resolve was weakening a little. Stacey could feel it. It was those damned puppy dog eyes and the tone of his voice. She stared at him for a few seconds. *He's a billionaire. He lives in a different world than you do. He wants to take away your home. How can you tell yourself that this is okay?*

Her inner dialogue was right, and Stacey knew it. As Charlie stared at her, she knew that she owed it to herself not to make any snap judgments. It would be so easy to forgive him and run back into his arms. He was there, living and breathing in front of her, wanting her forgiveness. When was the last time that had happened in her life?

Even so, he was still the tyrant trying to evict her. He had lied about who he was. No matter his reasons, the lie was still wrong.

"I can't. I'm sorry, Charlie," she finally whispered.

He looked crestfallen. For a couple of seconds, it looked as if all the air had been let out of him. His shoulders slouched forward. But it was only for a couple of seconds. Then Charlie straightened himself up. His poker face came back. His expression was unreadable.

"I understand, Stacey. Have a good night."

He turned around and walked away. For a moment, Stacey wanted to call out to him. For some reason, she was the one who was feeling shitty. Why? She had done the right thing. The look in his eyes came back to her, and she felt a wave of sadness wash over her.

Stacey stood there and watched Charlie cut across the parking lot toward his car. He didn't look back.

Chapter Twelve

"I need a favor."

"No."

Allison sighed and rolled her eyes. "Stacey, you don't even know what it is yet."

Stacey glanced up from the puny sandwich she was making for dinner. Her sister was leaning against the wall in the kitchen. Her arms were crossed. She had just painted her nails, and they glittered underneath the low light. Her features were tight, signaling to Stacey that whatever her favor was, she wasn't going to like it.

"Tell me so I can say no."

"Jacob is having this party on his yacht. He invited me."

"Okay—" Stacey said, not following.

"Well, he told me to invite any family or friends I wanted."

"You have no friends," she pointed out.

It was a bit harsh but was ultimately still the truth. Her sister had always been more concerned with snagging up the boys than making friends. She also tended to sleep with men who had girlfriends. It wasn't exactly shocking that Allison struggled to make friends.

"Well, he said family, too."

Stacey was about to finish making her sandwich when Allison's words made her freeze. She looked over her shoulder.

"Are you kidding me?"

"No," Allison replied quickly and hurried over to her side. "Come with me. Please. I don't want Jacob to think that I don't have anyone to bring. I want to look like I at least have a good relationship with my sister." She meant it as a joke but it came out harsh, and Stacey winced.

"Some high-end party? On a yacht? That isn't my scene at all. Besides, I probably have to work."

"No, it's this Saturday, and you don't. I checked," she remarked, pointing to Stacey's schedule she had stuck up on the fridge.

"I have nothing to wear. I have nothing to do there."

Allison gripped her arm. "Please. Seriously, I'm begging you. I'll sell the stupid tennis bracelet if you want me to."

This took Stacey by surprise, "What?"

"The bracelet." She shook her wrist in Stacey's face as if to jar her memory. "You said we'd get a lot of money, right? Well, if you come with me to this, I'll sell it."

She narrowed her eyes, "Why? You love that thing."

"Right, but if I snag Jacob, I'll have so many tennis bracelets that I won't need this one. Let me wear it to the yacht party, and then we can sell it, alright? But I need you to come with me. I need to have someone with me at the party. Jacob will think I'm weird if I don't take him up on his invite."

Stacey stared at the tennis bracelet, thinking about just how much money they could get with it. It would be worth it. Even if Jacob had given Allison subpar diamonds, the money would still be more than she currently had.

"Fine."

Allison's face lit up. "Amazing!" She threw her arms around Stacey and gave her a hug.

When the hug ended, her sister added, "Also, I think that asshole is going to be there. We could totally spit in his drink or something."

"Are we five?" Stacey asked before frowning. "Wait, which asshole?"

"That Charlie Albert guy," Allison replied as she grabbed a bag of chips out of the pantry. "He's going to be there. I figured we could do something. I don't know, stick a *kick me* sign on his back or something."

"Seriously, are we five?" She shook her head, still trying to digest the thought of seeing Charlie again.

"Well, what else do you want to do? Throw him off the boat?" Her sister paused as if it were a viable option, then shrugged. "Well, whatever. I'll help you plan an outfit, alright?"

She left the kitchen, humming a song to herself. Stacey watched her go and looked back down at her sandwich. She wasn't hungry anymore. She had been telling herself that she would be okay if she never saw Charlie again. Now, through her sister's schemes, she was going to see him again. On top of that, she was going to be completely out of her element.

"Great," she said aloud to no one.

"I'm so excited. Aren't you excited?"

"You've asked me this about fifty times in the last hour," Stacey grumbled.

Allison ignored her. They were in the car that Jacob had sent to pick them up. Yet Stacey couldn't help but be irritated that once again this guy hadn't come by to meet her sister directly. Was Allison being treated like Charlie had treated her? These billionaires apparently were fond of dating people far beneath their income level. It was probably some sort of game to them.

Not for the first time that night Stacey had found it funny that both she and her sister had ended up with a billionaire. While it wasn't shocking for Allison to be dating one, the fact that Stacey had also fallen into dating one was.

She still hadn't told Allison about it. She could almost hear the fight in her head play out. Her sister would simply ignore the fact that Stacey hadn't known who Charlie was. She would flip her shit over the fact that Stacey had been seeing the man responsible for their issues. She would then accuse her of *copying* off her lifestyle after judging her for it. It gave Stacey a headache just thinking about it.

To make matters worse, the money offered to vacate had been increased a couple of days ago. Stacey was sure this was directly related to what had happened with Charlie. The only thing she couldn't figure out was how he had meant it. Had he wanted to offer more money as an insult to them, knowing that it meant people would surely vacate? Or had he thought it would patch things up between them?

"Hello? Earth to Stacey!"

"Sorry," she said, snapping back to the present, "just not looking forward to this."

Allison rolled her eyes and leaned back in her seat. She was wearing a dress that Stacey had never seen before. She wasn't sure where her sister had gotten it. Stacey had dug out her nicest dress from the back of her closet. The last time she had worn it was when Jake had taken her out to dinner on their first anniversary. They had gone to a fondue place which had been way out of their budget. They had saved up for ages to go.

It had been strange slipping the dress back on. Stacey couldn't help but wonder how out of place she was going to feel. There were going to be rich people wearing designer clothes. While her own dress was nice, there was no way that it was going to be as lovely as the other outfits there.

If her sister was thinking the same thing, she didn't show it. That had always been yet another thing Stacey had been envious of. Allison never let anything shake her confidence. She could be attending a party in a garbage bag and would make it work.

"You aren't nervous?" Stacey couldn't stop herself from asking.

"Why would I be?"

"This isn't really our scene, is it? We are going to stick out like sore thumbs."

"How? We're invited by Jacob. Everyone will be too busy sucking up to him to give a shit about us," her sister said dismissively.

"Yeah, I guess so," Stacey responded unconvinced.

The car pulled up to the harbor in what felt like a couple of seconds. Stacey wished the drive had been longer, so she had more time to get emotionally ready. Who was she kidding? She wasn't going to feel ready no matter how long she had.

She moved to open the door, and Allison smacked her hand. "They'll get it."

Sure enough, the driver got out of the car and opened the door for Allison. She slinked out of the car with a smile plastered on her face. Then the driver went to the other side and opened the door for Stacey.

She stepped out into the summer air. Thankfully, it was cool tonight. The wind blew off the ocean and tempered the heat. It could have been enjoyable if she weren't so nervous.

The yacht was directly in front of them. She had never been on a boat of any size before. Seeing the sleek and massive yacht in front of them made Stacey feel very small. There was a group of people in front, waiting to be allowed on. Allison gripped her arm tightly and pulled her forward through the crowd.

They drew no attention. No one glanced their way. Everyone else seemed to know one another. No one cared about two no-names cutting through the crowd. Stacey was on high alert. She kept expecting to see Charlie appear at any moment. But there was no sign of him. She felt a mixture of both relief and disappointment.

"There you are!" Allison exclaimed, pitching her voice an octave higher.

Jacob came into view. He was taller than he looked in his photo and very skinny. He had long slim fingers that were holding a cigarette. His eyes were clear blue and his skin was so pale that he looked almost transparent.

He looked better in the grainy newspaper photo, Stacey thought as she slapped a phony smile on her face. She shook his hand, which felt clammy to the touch as if she was shaking hands with a dead trout rather than a man. *This* was the guy that Allison was trying so hard to woo? There was nothing remarkable about him. Stacey was sure that if he didn't have his money, no one would look twice at him.

"You made it. Wonderful," he said in a slight accent that Stacey couldn't pinpoint. "They're about to let us on board."

"Is this your yacht?" Stacey asked, trying to grasp for a topic of conversation.

"No, but it belongs to a close friend. Tony Lang owns it. You'll meet him soon enough."

"Great," Stacey said with an enthusiasm she wasn't feeling.

They boarded the yacht after a few minutes of waiting. Instantly, people fanned out across the deck. A live band was setting up on the bow. The doors to the interior were open, welcoming people inside. Stacey couldn't imagine what the cost of such a vessel was.

"I prefer the stern, actually," Jacob said as he looked around. "Less crowded."

Allison slipped her arm around his and beamed. "Then we'll go there. Lead the way."

Jacob took the hint and escorted her toward the rear of the yacht.

Seeing her sister so agreeable was cringe worthy. This was the same woman who used to throw a tantrum if Stacey sat on the right side of Tina's car instead of the left. Seeing her have no issue with following Jacob around was strange.

She trailed after them, quickly feeling as if she was turning invisible. With her eyes scanning the deck for Charlie, she tried to engage in conversation with Jacob and Allison. Yet Jacob seemed to never shut up. It became clear that his favorite topic of conversation was himself.

By the time they got to the stern, where a full bar had been set up, Stacey had decided she would try to get off the yacht before it launched. Allison had barely paid attention to her. She knew that her sister had wanted her along to look as if she was close with her family but now that Stacey had met Jacob, she doubted he cared. He had probably offered just to appear nice.

She was ready to turn around and head out when a handsome looking Asian man approached them.

"Tony!" Jacob said with more emotion than anything else he had said so far.

The two men shook each other's hands. Stacey assumed this was the owner of the yacht. As she stood next to her sister, she studied Tony. He was handsome. Next to Jacob, he looked like a male model. His skin was a lovely tanned shade that made Jacob look even more watery and sickly just standing next to him. His dark brown eyes looked almost black which fit well with his jet- black hair.

When he turned to look at Stacey and Allison, he had no accent at all when he introduced himself.

"I'm Allison. Jacob's date," her sister said, sticking out her hand to Tony. "This is my sister, Stacey."

"Lovely to meet you both," Tony replied, shaking her sister's hand.

Stacey held out her own to be polite. Instead of shaking it, however, Tony brought it up to his mouth and kissed the top of her hand very gently. Stacey was so startled that she yanked her hand away. She could feel a blush threaten to rise. If Tony noticed it, he was nice enough not to say anything.

"Well, if you will excuse me, I have to greet the other guests," he said, shooting one last smile at Stacey before heading off back into the crowd.

"He's nice," she said casually.

Allison shot her a knowing look, but all Jacob said was, "Yes. Actually—" and he launched into a boring diatribe about meeting Tony.

Stacey couldn't bother to pay attention. Especially because her heart felt as if it had stopped beating. Across from their small group was Charlie. He was by the railings and was looking directly at her. He had a drink in his hand and a strange look on his face. *Had he seen Tony kiss my hand? Or is he just surprised to see me here?* She convinced herself it didn't matter.

Seeing him was harder than she had expected. Even though the yacht was massive, it suddenly felt very small. She wanted to get out of there. Allison was draped over Jacob as he kept talking away. Two other people had appeared and were pretending to be interested as well.

Stacey took this as her cue to bail. With Charlie still staring at her, she turned around and began to weave her way through the crowd. She'd splurge and take a taxi home. She had shown up. That was enough to get the bracelet, right? She'd fight with Allison about that later.

Stacey finally got to where the ramp was to get off the yacht, but the plank was being pulled up. She shoved her way through a cluster of people and got the attention of a crewman.

"Sorry, I need to get off the boat."

"Sorry, ma'am. We're setting off in a few minutes."

"What? Are you sure you can't let me off this thing?"

The man looked at her apologetically. "I'm sorry, ma'am."

He walked away. Stacey stood there, staring at the dock. Sure enough, she could feel the engine come to life underneath her feet. There was a slight hum to the yacht that hadn't been there before. They were setting off, and she was stuck in a confined space with Charlie.

Chapter Thirteen

Stacey had been half expecting Charlie to appear at her side as soon as the yacht left the dock. But he was like a mirage. The crowd apparently swallowed him up, leaving Stacey alone.

She grabbed a flute of champagne from a passing waiter and found herself staring out at the water. It was strange to be there, on the deck of the ship. Life had been chaotic lately. Losing her job, worrying about an apartment, accidentally dating a billionaire—and now there she was, looking out at the ocean as she stood on a yacht.

The champagne was probably the nicest she had ever tasted before. She took another sip and glanced around the deck. No sign of Charlie. Perhaps she had a case of wishful thinking. She hated to admit it to herself, but maybe it would have been nice, to have Charlie seeking her out, chasing after her. It would have been a nice change of pace, to have her ego stroked.

"There you are!"

Her sister appeared at her side. Stacey was slightly surprised to see her. She was convinced that Allison had forgotten all about her.

"Hey. Just admiring the view." She decided to omit the fact she had been trying to get off the yacht.

"We're going in to eat with Tony in the saloon. Come on."

Stacey didn't get to protest. Allison had a firm grip when she wanted to. She pulled Stacey away from the railing and toward the saloon. She had been expecting something quaint and cozy. That was quickly proven wrong when they stepped inside.

The room looked as if it belonged to a penthouse. The floor had been cleared, and tables had been set up so guests could dine. There were servers everywhere, delivering plates brimming with food and refilling drinks. Everything was in varying shades of white. Art in golden frames hung on the walls. If it weren't for everything being bolted down, Stacey never would have guessed she was on a boat.

Allison dragged her toward one of the tables near the middle. Stacey automatically dug her heels into the carpet. Sitting at the table was Charlie.

"Oh look, that prick is here," her sister hissed quietly.

Stacey made a non-committal noise as she was shoved into a seat across from him at the end of the table. She stared down at her plate, wanting to avoid his gaze. Allison sat down on the other side of her, next to Jacob. Tony sat down next to Charlie with a beautiful woman that must have been either his wife or his date.

Jacob instantly dominated the conversation. Allison appeared to be hanging onto his every word. Stacey supposed this was why her sister was so good at snagging rich men. She was a great actress. Stacey could barely pretend to be interested.

At one point in the middle of a dull story, Charlie's eyes caught hers.

"The lion was right there," Jacob was droning on, "right by our jeep! He could have killed us, you know. We could have died right there on the spot if it decided to ravage us for a meal!"

Charlie smirked a little at her as if to say *this guy*. Stacey returned the smile, silently agreeing with him. Then, as if remembering they had broken up, she looked away, trying to wipe the smile off her face. What was she doing?

The meal they were served was delicious. Normally, she would have loved nothing more than eating such an amazing lobster. The presentation on the plate was gorgeous. But with Charlie being so close to her, she couldn't help but feel distracted.

He looked so handsome tonight. Glancing at him when she thought that he wasn't looking, Stacey could feel the longing in her chest. No matter how many times she told herself it was wrong, she couldn't help but want to reach out and grab him.

By the time dinner finished, Stacey couldn't have told anyone who asked what was discussed and if she had even engaged in conversation. As they wrapped up their meal, Tony turned to Charlie.

"You're awfully quiet tonight," he said to him. "Everything okay on your end?"

"Ah, yes. I have just a bit of a headache tonight. You know that I am prone to them." Charlie replied smoothly.

Tony went to open his mouth to reply when Jacob chimed up, "Have you tried peppermint tea? Might I suggest—"

Stacey tuned him out and stopped herself from rolling her eyes. Instead, she shot her sister a look. Allison gave her a small shrug as if to say *what do you want me to do with him?*

"Have you two seen the rest of the ship?" Tony asked, swiftly cutting Jacob's speech off.

"No, we haven't. Jacob, why don't you show me the rest?" Allison cooed.

Jacob looked placated at this after being interrupted. He nodded, and they both stood up from the table. Allison looked over at Stacey. Great. Either she went to be bored by Jacob or she was stuck there with Charlie. Which was the lesser of two evils?

She was saved from making any choice, however.

"I'm sure Tony or Charlie could show you around, sweet sister."

Sweet sister? Had Allison completely lost her mind? She couldn't recall any point in time that they had ever referred to each other like that. Jacob was smiling down at Allison though, so she supposed it was for his benefit. Gross.

"Uh, yeah, Sis. Sounds good."

"I'd be more than happy to show your sister around," Tony offered.

Tony's date looked a bit miffed at this. Stacey couldn't blame her. While she knew that this was his yacht, and he was just being kind, she was sure this beautiful woman wanted to spend time with him and not show another woman around. The woman said something in another language to Tony who replied in kind. Stacey couldn't understand any of it.

Charlie, possibly sensing the tension, came forward, "I'll show her. You have this entire party to tend to. I've been on here before." He smiled brightly.

"Ah, thanks so much," Tony replied. "I'll be seeing you around then? Nice speaking with you, Stacey."

They turned around and walked off. Stacey watched them leave and stood up from the table. At one point, Tony glanced behind him at the two of them. Stacey wiggled her fingers at him in a wave.

"Well, the stairs are this way."

"You're not actually going to show me around, are you?"

Charlie looked surprised. "You don't want to see the rest of the yacht?"

"I don't want to see it with you." She crossed her arms defensively.

"Well, no one else is going to show you around," he countered.

It was true. It wasn't as if she knew anyone else there. Allison had sauntered off with Jacob trying to woo him. Tony, while nice and admittedly lovely to look at, was off with his own date. Was she going to pass up seeing the rest of this place? She would never be near a yacht like this again in her life. She'd be kicking herself in six months when she remembered turning down seeing it because of Charlie.

"Fine. But conversation remains strictly about the yacht."

"Fine," he said, his features hardening slightly.

She followed him as he went to a door at the back of the saloon. Stacey hadn't noticed it before. It was carefully designed to look like part of the wall. The only way anyone could tell that it was different was because of the keypad next to it. Charlie pressed a few buttons, and the door clicked open.

"You know the code?"

"Tony and I go way back. I helped him out a while ago with some dealings in China."

"Kicking people out of their homes over there too?"

Charlie ignored her. She knew that he had heard her by the way he pressed his lips together. But all he did was open the door. A staircase was at their feet. It was narrow and steep, and Stacey balked at the idea of walking down it in her heels.

"Those look like stairs of death."

"These are the back steps to the cabins. The front staircase isn't much better."

"Why can't we use that one?"

"Everyone is using that one. We have this one all to ourselves. Listen, I'll go first. That way, in case you fall, you can snap my neck, and all your problems will be solved," he deadpanned.

Stacey wasn't sure if he was serious or joking. It was impossible to tell with his tone that dry. In any case, Charlie stepped down the staircase first. Stacey followed, moving so slowly down the steps that she was sure she heard him snicker at one point.

By the time he got to the bottom, she was only halfway down. He stuck his hands in his pockets and began to whistle. Had he always been this frustrating? Stacey got to the bottom of the stairs where they were now in a narrow hallway.

"Everything is so cramped."

"It's a boat."

"A massive one, so I assumed everything would be more normal sized."

"Hallways are narrow because the rooms are indeed massive. This back staircase leads us to the crew quarters, laundry room, a storage chamber, and a couple of cabins."

"And the front?"

"Access to the engine room and the master staterooms. Too crowded there right now. Tony really outdid himself there, so everyone wants to see them first."

"Great," she mumbled, feeling just how alone they were back there.

Everyone was either up front, upstairs, or on the deck. As she followed Charlie through the crew quarters and one of the smaller cabins, she couldn't help but feel nervous being this close to him.

While she had made it clear that she hadn't wanted to discuss anything but the yacht with him, being this close to him was affecting her. They were alone back there. Stacey could smell his cologne. She could recall how it felt when he had kissed her.

"This cabin is my favorite," he said, snapping her out of her memories.

Charlie pushed the door open, and they stepped inside. It was the smallest out of the other cabins that Stacey had seen so far but had the most décor. Everything had a soft pinkish hue to it. The carpet and the bed were in pastel shades of pink. The lamps on the night tables looked like giant seashells. There were more seashells painted along the wall.

"Sort of cheesy," she remarked. "None of the other rooms had this décor. Like, seashells? We're on a boat."

Charlie grinned, "Totally cheesy which is why I like it so much. Kinda campy, right? For a boat?"

She couldn't help but laugh. "You really like that? A boat having a beach theme?"

"Of course, I do," he said, running his hands over one of the seashell lamps. "Tony hates this room. But his late mother decorated it, and he leaves it like this in her memory. He changed the rest of the cabins except this one."

"Why does he hate it?"

"Because it's a corny seashell-themed room on a yacht. Way too on the nose for him."

"But you like it because of that very reason? Just to clarify."

"Yeah, exactly. It's cheesy. Sometimes cheesy can be a good thing. Tony said way back in the day having nautical themes on boats like this were the regular thing to do. But eventually, it fell out of fashion. People thought it was too corny. If I had a yacht, I'd have it all done up in a nautical theme. Too funny to pass up."

"I thought for sure you'd have a yacht," Stacey said.

"Nah. Not yet, anyway. The upkeep is crazy on a boat like this. If I got one, it'd be a smaller one."

"With a nautical theme."

Charlie grinned. "Definitely."

Stacey couldn't help but return the smile. Even though she had been so nervous only moments ago, the tension seemed to have faded. Now she felt exposed. They were close together in this cramped cabin. Stacey was feeling light-headed being this close to him.

Charlie seemed to sense it as well. He looked away from her and leaned against the wall of the cabin.

Stacey tried to find something to talk about, "You know, you can't even feel the engine. You would think we could feel the hum of the engine or something down here in the cabin," she rambled. "Something to indicate that you're out at sea. You know? It's sort of amazing, and I—"

She didn't get to finish her thought. Charlie took two swift steps closer and kissed her. His hands were against her cheeks as he cradled her face. Stacey was so shocked that her mind went completely blank for the first couple of seconds. Before she could stop herself, she was returning the kiss.

Then she remembered why she had broken things off with him and why it wouldn't work. With all the strength she could muster, she pushed away from him.

"We can't," Stacey whispered.

"Why not? I know you feel this. Why try to hide it? I even tried to make it right. I tried to offer more money."

"Charlie, I can't be bought!" She ran her fingers through her hair, feeling frustrated. "Why can't you see that? Offering more money isn't what I want. I want to stay where I live. I want to be there with my grandmother and my idiot sister and have enough money to take care of things and not live in the ghetto."

Charlie grabbed her hand. "Then I'll fix it."

"You can't. You can't, Charlie. We're too different, anyway."

"No, I'm going to fix it," he repeated, stubborn as ever.

Stacey was about to tell him yet again that he wasn't going to be able to fix this problem with more money. But his lips were on hers again. Just briefly. He ended the kiss after a couple of seconds and looked her in the eyes.

"I'm going to figure it out, okay?"

Stacey couldn't reply. Her throat had gone dry. She wanted to kiss him again, so very badly, that her entire body was aching. Part of her could picture tossing him down on the bed and taking him right there on the spot.

But she couldn't. As much as she wanted to, she couldn't. Charlie took her silence as a sign to go. He nodded once as if to himself and then left, leaving her alone in the cabin.

At that moment, with Charlie's lips still feeling as if they were pressed against hers, Stacey had never felt more alone.

Chapter Fourteen

"You didn't like him?"

"Oh, come on Allison," Stacey replied. "There is no way that you found Jacob at all interesting."

It was the day after the party. Stacey had just come home from a shorter shift than usual at the restaurant. Allison had her feet propped up on the coffee table and was painting her toenails a pale purple. Next to her was Tina, who was watching TV silently.

"You're right. I didn't. But so what?"

"You have to have some sort of connection with that guy."

"No, I don't. Besides, what about you?"

"What?" Stacey asked.

"Tony said Charlie showed you around the yacht. Why did you run off with the guy fucking us over?"

Stacey felt put on the spot. Her sister's glare was questioning yet her tone was slightly hostile. Part of her wanted to just admit the entire thing there and then. But she balked under the sudden gaze of her grandmother.

"You met the man in charge of the apartment deal?" Tina asked.

"Yeah, he was on the yacht last night," Allison replied. "So, come on, Stacey. What was he like?"

"Fine. He wasn't, uh, very interesting. Sort of droned on. Like Jacob. Guess that's just a billionaire thing," she said, standing up.

"Well, they all love talking about themselves. It's in their nature."

Stacey excused herself and headed off to the kitchen. Sure, Jacob talked about himself absolutely non-stop, but Charlie wasn't like that. She kept telling herself that she wasn't going to have to see him again but how could she be so sure? And what had he meant by saying he was going to fix things?

She grabbed a soda out of the fridge and opened it as Allison came into the kitchen. She was walking funny, trying not to smudge her freshly painted toenails.

"So, what's next for you and Jacob?" Stacey asked.

"Not sure. Just waiting for him to call me, I guess. He's going to Europe next week. Maybe he'll invite me."

"Yeah, maybe," Stacey said, unconvinced that Jacob was interested in her sister in any way other than a fling.

"Hand me a soda?"

"Here," she said, shoving her own can toward Allison. "I need to stop drinking this junk anyway."

There was a knock on the door. "I'll get it," said Stacey as she headed over to open it.

Charlie stood there. He was dressed plainly, in just a black t-shirt and a pair of jeans. She had never seen him dressed like that before. The sight of him made her mouth go dry. She glanced behind her. Tina was oblivious, still watching TV. Allison would be trailing into the living room in any second.

Stacey stepped out into the apartment hallway and closed the door behind her. "What are you doing here?"

"I need you to sign something. All the tenants are signing it."

"What?" she asked as he handed her paperwork.

"You can take some time to go over it. I don't need it back right away."

"What is it, Charlie?" Stacey repeated.

"My company is pulling out of the city expansion. This is just a formal notice that we aren't going to be asking anyone to vacate anymore."

Her head spun. She thought that he was poking fun at her. Surely, he had to be. Stacey was speechless and could only stare at him.

Charlie cleared his throat and avoided her gaze as he spoke, "So you'll want to review it before signing.

Someone will be by in a few days to pick it up. Everyone else has had theirs delivered."

"Wait. Wait, I'm sorry." She held a hand up. "What happened? I mean, what about that big speech you gave? About how this was what this city needed?"

"I still do think that. But the city needs it for everyone. We're shifting our focus. Improving public buildings with the assistance of the local government. Improving the parks, things like that. Your landlord will be instructed to start making repairs here as well."

"This is crazy. I don't even—" She pressed her hand to her forehead as if that would stop how fast her head was racing. "I don't know what to say."

Charlie lowered his voice, "Stacey, I promised I'd fix everything. This is how I'm fixing them. I couldn't ask you to leave your home. But I also couldn't save just your apartment complex, right? I could just hear you in my head telling me that sure, I helped you, but what about everyone else?"

"True. That is exactly what I would say," Stacey admitted, "but from the business side of things—how did you do this? How did you manage to swing this?"

"I work quickly and talk even faster." Charlie shrugged as if it was normal to restructure a plan like this so swiftly. "You're right. I did care more about rich people coming in and buying up high rises. But I didn't want to be like that. I didn't want to be like—"

"Like Jacob?" she asked helpfully.

Charlie laughed. His laugh was contagious, and she couldn't help but laugh as well. The situation was too strange not to be funny. A billionaire had just changed his business plan and saved her from having to move out of her apartment complex. It sounded like something out of a movie.

"Why did you do it?" she asked after she had caught her breath from laughing.

"You mean you don't know?" He brushed her cheek gently with his thumb, tilting her chin to look up at him.

Stacey held her breath. She wanted to lean forward and feel him on her lips, but she held off. If Allison or her grandmother were to open the door right now, there would be no explaining something like this. Even so, it was tempting.

"For you, Stacey. I wanted to see if you'd give me another chance if I made this right."

"For me?" She breathed, their lips only an inch away, hovering close, but not touching.

"That's right," Charlie whispered, "for you. If you give me another chance, I'd love to start over. Try us again, do it the right way, with no lies."

Stacey couldn't believe what was happening. What incredible influence Charlie must have to change everything so quickly. She couldn't imagine having so much power and so much respect that he could change a major business plan so fast.

It dawned on her then just who Charlie was. He was a billionaire. He could buy her whole city block if he wanted to, and still be a billionaire.

Yet he wanted *her*. Stacey had told him that they were too different, that their socio-economic backgrounds were worlds apart for a relationship to work. She had made it clear she couldn't be with the man who was trying to evict her and her neighbors from their apartment complex. And Charlie hadn't left. Instead, he had changed everything with the hope for another shot with her.

"I'll have you," she whispered.

Charlie's lips finally found hers. This kiss sent goosebumps up and down her arms. It was a short kiss—neither one of them wanted to get caught making out in the hallway. But before they parted, Charlie spoke.

"When are you free next? Let me take you to dinner."

"I'm free Wednesday night."

"So far away." He ran his thumb over her lips. "Guess I'll just have to wait then."

He pulled away from her. Stacey watched him leave. He went down the stairs and disappeared from her view in a matter of seconds. Her heart raced so quickly that she felt dizzy for a couple of seconds. She looked down at the papers in her hand. *We aren't going to have to leave,* she thought to herself with a thrill.

The door opened, and Allison stuck her head out. "What in hell are you doing out here?"

Stacey turned around to face her sister who was looking at her perplexed. She held the papers out to her.

"I think everything just got fixed," was all she said.

Wednesday morning, Stacey woke up with a light heart. Today she was going to see Charlie. He was going to pick her up at six. She couldn't wait. All she had to do was get through a short shift at work and be home in time to get ready.

She was still on the fence about telling her sister about him. She had come close the last couple of days but had been holding back for some reason. It wasn't as big of a deal now since they were going to be staying in the apartment complex.

Word had spread around the city like wildfire. The fact that a large company had made such a sudden change was big news. Residents were pleased they could stay in their homes. They were happy they would be seeing improvements to the city that catered to everyone and not just the wealthy. Charlie's face had been splashed on the front page of the newspaper almost daily in the past few days.

So, it would have made sense to tell Allison and Tina what was going on between her and Charlie. Even so, Stacey had been holding back. Besides the fact she knew Allison would still judge her for it, she also wanted to keep it to herself. For some reason, having Charlie to herself made it feel more like a special secret that she could enjoy on the sly, without sharing. Too often in the past, she had introduced Allison to the men she had liked. It had always seemed to jinx things.

No, she had decided that Charlie was going to be her little secret. She had already told Allison she was seeing Amanda later that night. Her sister had barely noticed. She was too upset about Jacob not inviting her to Europe.

"How could this be happening? I thought for sure he had loved spending time with me at that party," Allison bemoaned as Stacey tried not to roll her eyes.

"He loves himself more," she remarked.

Allison ignored her. "I thought I was going to get to go to Europe for sure."

"Maybe he's going there on business and didn't want to invite you. Have you even considered that?"

"Doesn't matter. If he were into me, he would have invited me. We could have sealed the deal in Europe."

"And what? Been his full-time mistress?"

Allison scowled. "Don't start."

"I'm just saying that you should aim higher instead of trying to snag a billionaire."

"God, not this again, please. Not now. I have to rethink this."

Stacey poured herself some cereal. Tina was still asleep when Stacey checked up on her earlier. As her sister rambled in the background, Stacey thought of her grandmother. She had been sleeping more than usual lately. Besides raising her voice at the two sisters when they had been bickering before, Tina had been quiet as ever. Stacey was sure it was because her memory was growing worse. Tina probably couldn't keep up with simple conversations.

Now that there was no threat of moving, Stacey decided she would take Tina to the doctor again sooner rather than later. It had been too long since Tina had gone due to money issues. It was time for a check-up.

"Are you even listening?" Allison asked.

"No," Stacey replied, sitting down at the table. "No, sorry, I don't really care. Listen, don't get all huffy with me because that boring twig of a man didn't invite you to Europe." Something struck her—something she had forgotten with everything going on. "Where is the tennis bracelet, by the way? You promised to use it to help with the bills."

"Oh. Yeah—" A funny look crossed her sister's face.

Stacey braced herself, in case Allison's explanation caused her to get upset just as she was about to head out to work. She could feel it in her gut. The cereal suddenly looked unappealing, and she pushed the bowl away.

"What did you do?"

Allison tried to look insulted. "Why is it me?"

"What, did someone steal it?"

"Well, no."

"Then what did you do?" Stacey repeated icily.

"I gave it back to him."

"Why?!"

"I thought it was romantic!" Allison exclaimed as Stacey got up from the table. "I told him I'd be waiting for him and I'd take the bracelet back when he came back for me. I told him to take it and keep it to remind him of me."

"Allison, why not give him something of *yours*, you complete and total fool?" Stacey snapped as she marched to the front door. "What is he going to do with something he gave you not even a week ago?"

"He doesn't want something of mine, Stacey, he wants diamonds and expensive things. It just made sense to give him the bracelet. Listen, when he comes back for me, I'll get it—"

"Save it, alright?"

Stacey stormed out of the apartment, slamming the door loudly behind her. Leon was in the doorway of his mother's apartment, idly texting on his phone.

"Hey, Stacey," he said to her. "Heard the good news?"

"Yes." She forced a smile on her face, trying to mask her irritation at her sister. "Fantastic, isn't it?"

"Sure is. Guess even the rich assholes can come around, huh?"

"You should watch your mouth, Leon," Stacey lectured, partly because of his age and partly because he was insulting Charlie.

"Sure, sure. Have a good day," he said before looking back down at his phone.

Stacey walked past him and headed down the stairs. She was trying not to be angry at Allison, but that was proving to be impossible. She had been so close to having some actual money coming in, and her sister had blown it trying to impress that idiot.

Downstairs, a woman stood in the lobby. It was clear that she had no place in the housing complex. She was wearing a sleek, pure white dress that hugged every curve. Her hands were wrapped around a purse that was just as white. Her heels were black and matched her jet-black hair that was thrown up in a perfectly messy bun that was the style of the day. She had giant sunglasses on that covered half her face. The only bit of color on her was her red lips.

"Hi, are you lost?" Stacey asked, knowing that everything on this woman was designer made and wondering how she had ended up walking in there of all places.

"Yes, I believe so. I'm looking for someone." She had a light accent, but her tone was clipped, making it clear she didn't want to talk to Stacey any longer than necessary.

"Who are you looking for?"

"Charlie Albert. He had business here before he mucked up the deal. Have you seen him?"

Stacey's heart began to beat quickly. "Uh, no. No, not for a few days. Who are you?" It was a bit blunt, but she couldn't help herself. Who was this woman?

The woman lowered her glasses and looked over the frames. Her eyes were a bright green. Her gaze made Stacey feel insignificant.

"I'm Charlie Albert's fiancée, not that it's any business of yours."

-To be continued in Book 2-

If you enjoyed this title, I would appreciate your leaving a review of the book. Good reviews encourage an author to write as well as help books to sell. Good reviews can be just a few short sentences describing what you liked about the book without having a spoiler. If you could spend 30 seconds writing a review, I would appreciate it: you can review this title right now at your favorite retailer.

Here is a preview of the **next book** you may also enjoy:

Love Divested: Persuasive Billionaire BWWM Romance Series, Book 2

DOWNSTAIRS IN the lobby, Stacey saw a woman who was, clearly, not a tenant. The stranger looked like she belonged in a fashion magazine.

Trying to be helpful, Stacey asked, "Hi, are you lost?"

The woman looked Stacey up and down before answering. "Yes, I believe so. I'm looking for someone."

"Who are you looking for?"

"Charlie Albert. He had business here before he mucked up the deal. Have you seen him?"

Stacey's heart raced. "Uh, no. No, not for a few days. Who are you?" It was a bit blunt, but she couldn't help herself. Who was this woman?

The woman lowered her glasses and replied, "I'm Charlie Albert's fiancée, not that it's any business of yours."

Stacey thought she misheard the woman. There had to be some sort of mistake. There was no way that this woman was Charlie's fiancée.

"I'm Adele," the woman went on, oblivious to Stacey's inner turmoil. "I wanted to surprise him, you see. I've been overseas. His assistant said he had been here a couple times, so I thought he could be here now."

"Sorry, he hasn't been here since the apartments were dropped from the rebuilding plan." Stacey hoped her voice sounded as if she had no interest in Adele or her claims of being Charlie's fiancée.

Adele wrinkled her nose. "That's a shame. I suppose I'll try him elsewhere then. Now that I'm here, though, I can understand why he would leave as quickly as possible." She laughed.

Stacey wanted to tell this strange, uppity woman that this was her home. She didn't need strangers coming around running their mouths off about how little they thought of it. But she couldn't bring herself to say anything. Instead, she could only stare at Adele, who was looking around the lobby one last time.

"Well, thank you for the help, dear," Adele said and left the apartment complex in her towering high heels without a backward glance.

Stacey just stood there. Her head was spinning as if everything had suddenly been uprooted. Part of her wanted to chase after Adele and ask her just how she could be Charlie's fiancée.

But a sick, swooping feeling was slowly consuming Stacey. She had to talk to Charlie as soon as possible. She fumbled for her phone and brought up his number. The phone rang three times before a man answered.

"Charlie Albert's phone." The man's voice was deep and somehow familiar although it wasn't Charlie.

No one had ever picked up Charlie's cell phone before and it threw Stacey off guard. She stumbled over her words. "Hi, uh, hello. This is Stacey, and, um, I'm Charlie's—" What was she, exactly? His girlfriend? Or just a girl on the side?

"Stacey!" the man exclaimed as if he knew her. "This is Tony."

In her haze, it took her a few seconds to remember who Tony was. The image of him smiling at her on board his yacht floated back to Stacey.

"Right, hi Tony!" She feigned a cheerfulness. "How are you? Your yacht was very lovely."

"Glad you enjoyed it. I enjoyed seeing you on it."

The remark startled her. His tone had been warm and almost flirtatious. That's odd, she thought to herself.

"I'm calling for Charlie," she blurted out and cringed.

She probably sounded incredibly rude. She was blowing off what Tony had just said. But Stacey had no idea what to make of it and couldn't focus on that right now. The image of smug Adele still danced in her memory.

"He's in a meeting. He's running late, actually, because we had a meeting of our own. That's how I have his phone," Tony joked, "but I can pass him a message."

"Yeah, please. Let him know I called and would appreciate a call back."

"Of course. I had no idea you two were so, well, close," Tony replied tactfully.

For one wild second, Stacey wanted to ask Tony about Adele. He would know, wouldn't he? Tony and Charlie seemed to be friends and ran in the same social circles. But she stopped herself before she could do something so silly. No, whatever was going on was something she would ask Charlie directly. She would not go behind his back.

"Thank you! I have to go to work now. Have a nice day!" Her voice was too high-pitched as she tried to hide her emotions. It just made her sound crazy and somewhat desperate.

She ended the call and headed to work, telling herself that she would get to the bottom of it soon enough.

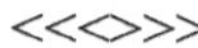

Although Stacey had promised herself not to dwell on Charlie and Adele, it proved to be impossible. The restaurant had one lone customer—an old lady sitting at a booth asking for coffee non-stop as she read a book.

Maria bustled into the kitchen about two hours into her shift and looked over at Stacey. "I quit."

"What? That just leaves me and Amanda."

Maria shrugged. "Not my problem. I'm going to go fucking mental if I stay here a second longer. See you around."

Stacey stared as Maria headed toward the break room. She hadn't ever been exactly close with Maria so she hadn't been expecting a tearful goodbye. But a mumbled 'see you around' was a pretty shitty farewell.

Tears formed in Stacey's eyes. She turned away to face the wall. *What is wrong with me?* She tried to regroup. Normally, someone quitting wouldn't affect her like this.

She left the kitchen, leaving Brad behind playing a game on his phone and found William in his office. She knocked on the door, and he looked up at her.

"You're not quitting too, are you? I was hoping to run with a skeleton crew until we closed, but it's turning more into a ghost crew at this point."

"Nope, I'm here 'til we close," Stacey replied. "I have a job lined up afterward already."

"Amanda mentioned that the other day. Congrats."

Working at another diner didn't seem like something to be congratulated about. Out of the blue, her sister's words from their last fight haunted her. *All you do is work at some dead-end job without ever trying to better yourself or move onto something new.*

If you enjoyed this sample then look for **Love Divested: Persuasive Billionaire BWWM Romance Series, Book 2.**

Here is a preview of **another story** you may enjoy:

Love Deceived: Tenacious Billionaire BWWM Romance Series, Book 1

"**I LIKE** your buns." The customer's voice was creamy, with a hint of spice. "How much are they?"

"Excuse me?" Adalia glanced up from behind the cash register and glared at the man.

"Your buns," he answered, flashing a naughty grin at her.

Heat erupted in her core.

It was him. The guy. He came in every day in that Prada suit, no suitcase, and flaunted his perfect jawline and wavy blond hair. Adalia's stomach did a turn, but she steadied herself mentally.

Come on, it's just a customer. Same as any other in the bakery.

"Can I help you with something?" She asked the same question each day when he came in. Then it would begin.

"That depends." The gorgeous man strolled over and rested his elbows on the glass of the counter that displayed treats and sweets.

"On what, exactly? It's pretty simple," she answered. "Either you want the buns or you don't."

"Oh," he replied, interlocking his fingers and resting his chin on them. "I want the buns. You can count on that." He reached out and brushed her forearm with the tips of his fingers. Sparks danced across her ebony skin.

Adalia cleared her throat gently, but didn't move away. It was the first time he'd touched her, and she'd honestly fantasized about the moment for weeks.

"Which buns would you like?" She breathed the words, and he leaned in close enough that she caught a whiff of his cologne. It was a masculine, woody scent and it suited him perfectly.

Warning alarms went off in her head – this guy was clearly a player, well put together, with that easy charm – but they were drowned out by her attraction to him.

"Yours," he uttered, "every day, for the next month. Every night, too."

Adalia narrowed her chocolate brown eyes at him. She'd given up trusting anyone a long time ago, let alone suave white strangers with a clear desire for more than a carb fix.

"I wouldn't advise you eat that many carbs. And you've yet to specify which type of buns you'd like, sir." She gave a sweet smile she didn't feel in her gut.

Why couldn't she shake her attraction to this guy? She'd just gotten out of a relationship with DeShawn, just started the healing process. She had to focus on getting the bakery on track, not on some sexy dude with a fetish for curvy women.

God, wouldn't it be nice if he had a fetish for – No!

He studied her expression with a grin that made her insides go melty like tempered chocolate.

"I think you know which buns I want."

"Cinnamon," she answered, reaching over for a brown paper bag beneath the glass fronted cabinet. In the back, one of her bakers slammed a tray in the oven and cursed.

Irritation flickered through her – they never treated those ovens with respect – but she kept a straight face.

"No, no," he answered, then grasped her wrist again, and heat waves assaulted her. "I'm in the mood for chocolate today."

She stared him dead in the eye, willing the arousal to back the hell down. "Smooth," she said wryly.

"Excuse me, miss. I'd like to pay?" said a hunched over granny, clasping a box of éclairs.

"Sorry, ma'am," Adalia replied, sparing a frown for the handsome businessman. He winked a blue eye at her and she swallowed hard. "That will be five dollars."

"Five dollars," the lady answered, squinting a little and stretching to pat her curlers. Adalia glanced at 'Handsome Guy' again. He hadn't looked away, and their gazes were glued for a moment. "I'll tell you, it's a pity these éclairs are so good, dearie. You're going to have me on the streets at this rate."

"I'm glad you like them," Adalia replied. That was the plain truth: with the bills piling up, every happy customer helped pave the pathway to financial success. Losing her lifelong dream wasn't an option. "Can I get you anything else?"

"Oh no, dear. Perhaps the recipe so I can make these for myself at home." The old woman's wrinkled façade split into a friendly smile. "No, I'm joking, of course. I quite enjoy the trip into the city for these treasures." She lifted one from the bag and took a bite. Cream squished out the sides and smeared onto her cheek.

"I'll get you a napkin." Adalia fumbled for them beside the register, but Handsome Guy was already on it.

He swept out a handkerchief and handed it to the customer with a courteous bob of his head.

"Thank you," the lady breathed, accepting it with a flutter of her eyelids. "My, what a dashing young fellow. You certainly are a lucky woman." She directed that at Adalia.

"What? He's not my –"

"Not as lucky as I am," he put in, and gestured for the customer to keep the soft square of linen. She thanked him and shuffled out with a cheery wave, pink slippers slapping on the linoleum.

Adalia had given the bakery a fifties' style look. She'd loved the idea of a parlor where customers could sit and have a milkshake while they ate their baked goods. So far, the idea hadn't taken off.

The booths and chairs were empty. A pang of regret stabbed at her stomach, and she wiped down her flowered apron with a grimace.

"I'll get those chocolate buns for you," she said to the businessman, but the stare he gave her made her stop dead in her tracks. "What is it? You don't want them anymore?"

"I do, but I'd prefer it if you had a few with me. Do you make coffee here?"

"We do," she said, "but I've got way too much to do to take a break."

"I wasn't asking."

"Look, I don't even know your name. What makes you think you can come in here, flirt with me and make a fool out of me in front of my customers?" Adalia allowed anger to gutter through her and override the desperate need to reach out and spank that cute butt. "Now, if you want buns, I'll give you buns, but I'm going to have to ask you to leave."

"I assume you don't normally treat your customers this way." He glanced left and right, searching the empty storefront with mock intrigue.

If you enjoyed this sample then look for **Love Deceived: Tenacious Billionaire BWWM Romance Series, Book 1**.

Here is a preview of **another story** you may enjoy:

Love Disrupted: Ardent Billionaire Romance Series, Book 1

DEIRDRE CLARKE stepped out of her apartment into the hot Los Angeles sun; dusk had fallen, but the temperature still sat near 100 degrees. Deirdre was already running late for her gig, so the sight of her ex-boyfriend Carl standing by her car irritated her even more than usual. She stomped down the single flight of stairs and greeted him with hostility.

"I'm late. What the hell do you want?" Deirdre demanded.

"Can't a man just stop by to see his best girl?" Carl smiled. His green eyes complimented his mocha skin and for a moment Deirdre forgot why she'd put up with his shit for so long. Then she remembered why she'd stopped.

"I guess you'd better go see her then," she said roughly. "And let me be on my way."

"Dee… you know I'm talking about you."

"I'm not your girl no more," she answered, "and I've got somewhere to be."

"Don't be mad, Dee I just came here to check on you… you alright? What about D'Angelo? You two need anything? You got rent covered?"

Deirdre's blood boiled and she met his eyes with a defiant stare. "I don't need a damn thing from you. D'Angelo and I are not your business anymore." Deirdre had been responsible for her younger brother since their mother had gone to prison. D'Angelo was one of the reasons she'd known she had to get away from Carl in the first place. The last thing she wanted was for her brother to see her thug ex-boyfriend as a role model.

"When are you going to understand that you can't buy your way back here?" She glared at him.

"Deirdre, we were together almost our whole lives. I love you. But I'm not trying to buy my way back. I have a business proposition for you."

"I don't need a job, I have two," she snapped, trying to open her car door. Carl blocked her way.

"Its easy money Dee… you wouldn't even know it was here."

"Ah, I see. You think I'll hide drugs or hot shit for you, after all of the hell you put me through? You think I'd take that risk for you and your 'boys'?" She snorted back at him.

"It's just herb, Dee… it's practically legal. And I don't know why you're so pissed at me. Nothing that went down was my FAULT!"

"Our windows were SHOT OUT, Carl. You can stand there all you want and claim it was a random drive-by, swear it wasn't personal, but I'm not a moron! You think I didn't know you'd fallen in with Derrick and his thugs? You think I believed your lies about where all the money was coming from? I KNEW what you were doing, and you just denied, denied, denied.

Until our home was shot up... with my brother inside. Take your shit and get out of my face." Deirdre shoved him out of the way of her car and escaped inside. She checked her face in the rearview mirror, and then prayed she'd have time to fix her make-up before she had to go onstage.

She stood on stage, in her element. As Lou played along on the black grand piano, Deirdre let all of her emotions flow out to the music. The small crowd gave her their undivided attention as she belted out Trouble, Stormy Weather, and Summertime. Her white, full length gown stood in stark contrast to the milk-chocolate color of her skin.

Deirdre couldn't remember a time when she didn't love to sing. When she was still a young girl, before her father left, her family went to church every Sunday. She loved listening to the soloists in the choir and dreamed of one day standing next to them. But they'd stopped going to church once her father was gone. When D'Angelo was born, Deirdre had tried to get her mother to go back, but she'd refused; D'Angelo's father was against the idea. But soon, he was gone too. Looking back, Deirdre was sure that was when her mother started using drugs, though she didn't realize what was happening at the time. Three years ago, right after Deirdre graduated from high-school, Pauline Clarke had been busted and sentenced to twenty years in a federal prison. Deirdre became D'Angelo's legal guardian, though in all honesty she'd raised him since he was born.

D'Angelo was a good kid, especially considering everything he'd been through. And he was the reason Deirdre hadn't fallen into the same kind of traps the other girls in her neighborhood had found themselves in. She hadn't had any kids, she hadn't gotten messed up on drugs, and she didn't take her clothes off for money. Instead, Deirdre worked as a hotel maid and took college courses online. She'd have loved to go to school on an actual campus, but she couldn't afford childcare for D'Angelo and she refused to turn him into a latchkey kid at eight years old. Deirdre worked while he was at school, and then after dinner they did their homework together.

Thursday nights were different. Those nights were all for Deirdre. She had a standing gig at Fuseli's, an upscale jazz club in the Hollywood foothills. The gig paid just enough for Deirdre to afford her stage-clothes, but she didn't do it for the money.

When she finished her last set, Deirdre took a seat at the bar and ordered herself a beer and a sandwich. As the bartender walked towards the tap, a tall, broad stranger signaled his attention. When he returned to Deirdre, he carried a martini with her draft.

"Dee, a kind gentleman asked me to bring you this and wondered if you'd mind some company?"

Deirdre looked up at Steve and sighed. After her encounter with Carl, she was in no mood to put up with anyone's advances. "Tell him thank you, but I can't possibly accept."

"I don't know… this one's pretty hot, Dee… he's the one down there, in the suit."

"Really Steve, I'm not up for it right now."

"Alright, fine…" he answered in a disapproving, sing-song voice.

Deirdre thought the issue was dealt with as she watched Steve approach the end of the bar to deliver the message. The gorgeous blonde man took the martini, rose, and headed Deirdre's way.

"I'm sorry," she began as he approached, frustrated that he wouldn't take a hint.

"No, I'm sorry." He smiled. "Your friend told me you've had a bad day. You sang beautifully… I sent this as a token of my appreciation, nothing more," he explained, raising the drink. "Why don't you enjoy it? It might make you feel better. Or I could buy you something else, if you'd prefer? Right before I return to my seat, of course."

If you enjoyed this sample then look for **Love Disrupted - Ardent Billionaire Romance Series, Book 1**.

Other Books by Shyla Starr

- Tenacious Billionaire BWWM Romance Series

- Elusive Billionaire Romance Series

- Lonely Billionaire Romance Series

- Ardent Billionaire Romance Series

- Fervent Billionaire BWWM Romance Series

- Audacious Billionaire BWWM Romance Series

Get the latest update on new releases from the author at:

https://shylastarr.com/newsletter/

About the Author - Shyla Starr

Shyla currently specializes in writing interracial romance stories and is a huge fan of the alpha male. Simply put, there just aren't enough stories about mixed couple romances, which is something she is aiming to fix.

Being a bookworm all her life, when Shyla discovered men she also realized how easy it was to fulfill her fantasies through her writing.

When not writing and fantasizing about men, Shyla enjoys dancing, reading and chilling with her friends.

Connect with Shyla Starr

I really appreciate you reading my book! Here are my social media coordinates:

Friend me on Facebook:
https://www.facebook.com/shylastarrauthor

Follow me on Twitter: https://twitter.com/shylstarr

Check me out on Goodreads:
https://www.goodreads.com/author/show/8436084.Shyl a_Starr

Subscribe to my newsletter:
https://shylastarr.com/newsletter/

Visit my website: https://shylastarr.com/